"Who are you?" he demanded

The urge to hit him in the face with it was strong. "I'm Beth Delaney," she shot at him. It gave Beth savage satisfaction to see he hadn't completely forgotten her. "I came looking for Jamie."

His chin jutted. A muscle in his cheek flinched.

"He once said he would come to me when he could. He never did. Last night I had the chance to look him up. But Jamie was gone. I only found Jim Neilson."

His mouth thinned into a grim line.

"Now it's time for Beth Delaney to go, too," she said with bleak finality. "There's nothing left of what there once was."

She turned away. There was nothing to hold her here. No doubt Jim Neilson would only feel intense relief at seeing her go, a ghost from the past he didn't want to remember.

"Wait."

The snapped sh across her sho

EMMA DARCY nearly became an actress, until her fiancé declared he preferred to attend the theater with her. She became a wife and mother. Later, she took up oil painting—unsuccessfully, she remarks. Then she tried architecture, designing the family home in New South Wales, Australia. Next came romance writing—"the hardest and most challenging of all the activities," she confesses.

Books by Emma Darcy

HARLEQUIN PRESENTS

EMMA DARCY

Craving Jamie

Harlequin Books

TORONTO • NEW YORK • LONDON
AMSTERDAM • PARIS • SYDNEY • HAMBURG
STOCKHOLM • ATHENS • TOKYO • MILAN
MADRID • WARSAW • BUDAPEST • AUCKLAND

ISBN 0-373-11881-3

CRAVING JAMIE

First North American Publication 1997.

Copyright © 1997 by Emma Darcy.

CHAPTER ONE

SHE wore yellow.

It was the colour that first drew Jim Neilson's eye. A daffodil amongst black orchids, he thought whimsically. Women in the arty crowd always seemed to wear black—leather, satin, silk, slinky knits—dressed up with gold chains or exotic costume jewellery. It was like a uniform that said, "I fit in. I belong to this smart, classy world." The gallery was full of them, come to see or be seen at the preview of Paul Howard's exhibition.

Jim wore black, too—silk shirt, designer jeans, casual leather jacket, Italian shoes. He quite enjoyed the illusion of fitting in, even while knowing he didn't and never would. The sense of apartness never left him, no matter how high he climbed on the various ladders he'd chosen. In this milieu he had a well-earned reputation as an art collector. His opinion was respected, his favour sought. But that didn't make him fit. It simply meant he had money to spend.

The woman in yellow intrigued him. She obviously didn't mind standing out, being different. Not many people could wear that particular colour successfully. It either sallowed the skin or was too dominant, washing out the person. On her, it looked stunning. Just a simple linen suit with clean, classic lines.

She carried herself like a model, tall, slim, shoulders straight to maximise the striking curves of her figure, a long neck to support the thick fall of silky caramel hair that dropped to below her shoulders. Her face had an appealing, natural look, the golden tan of her smooth skin shining with vitality rather than matted with make-up. Bright eyes, a lush mouth and a straight, aristocratic nose.

Quite a honey, Jim thought, sexual interest aroused. His love-life—if it could be called that— could do with a boost. His interest in Alysha had waned even before she flew off for the fashion shows in Europe. He wanted someone new. A woman who excited him.

There were several women here who would jump at the chance of a tumble in bed with Jim Neilson. They didn't care about the person he was inside, though. Just fancied him. Or what he could offer. He was bored with shallow relationships. He craved something more. A bit of mystery? The spur of a hunt instead of a lay-down gift?

The woman in yellow looked like a bright splash of spring in this crowd of sophisticates. Fresh. Tantalising. Whoever she was, she seemed to be alone, no one closely tagging her. She didn't speak to anyone, either. His curiosity was more and more piqued as he watched her.

She wasn't interested in the paintings. Her gaze only skimmed them, no pause for any lengthy assessment of their value or attraction to her personally. She looked at the men in each group she passed, scanning them closely as though anxious not to miss a face. The women were ignored, apparently inconsequential to her.

"Another glass of champagne, Jim?"

Claud Meyer at his elbow, oiling his way to a sale. The owner of the fashionable Woollhara gallery was always an assiduous host to good clients. This cocktail-hour preview would probably result in enough purchases to ensure the exhibition's success for both artist and entrepreneur. Claud was a good businessman. Jim respected that while seeing straight through the tactics being used.

"Why not? Thank you," he said, setting his empty glass on the silver tray Claud held and picking up a full one. "Quite a turnout tonight."

"Popular artist," was the knowing reply. "See anything you like?"

"Yes." He nodded towards her. "The woman in yellow."

Claud's surprise was quickly swallowed into a good-humoured chuckle. "I meant the landscapes on show."

"The guy has talent, but there's nothing that hits me in the eye and says, 'Buy me!'"

"He'll be a good investment," came the swift persuasion.

"Who is she?"

Claud followed the line of his gaze then looked back, puzzled. "Are you kidding me?"

"You must know who she is, Claud. This preview is by invitation only."

He frowned. "I've never seen her before in my life. She didn't have an invitation. I let her in because she said she was meeting you."

Jim's curiosity took a mega-leap. "How very enterprising of her," he mused.

"I assumed since you came alone..."

"She was my date?"

Claud shifted uneasily, not enjoying being wrong-footed. "If she lied..."

"No. Let her be, Claud. She will be meeting me." Jim eyed the gallery owner with a sardonic twinkle. "If she likes one of these landscapes, I might even buy it. Who knows what could eventuate?"

Recognising there was no profit in engaging Jim Neilson in further conversation, Claud smiled and said, "In that case, I hope she pleases both of us."

"Mind if I take another glass of champagne?"

"Help yourself."

Claud moved on, doing the rounds of prospective customers. Jim concentrated his attention on the woman in yellow. Had she tossed off his name simply as a ploy to get into the gallery, or was it her intent to meet him? For what purpose? It was an intriguing question.

Was she a gold-digger on the hunt? Ever since he'd been listed as one of the most eligible bachelors in Australia—without his permission—he'd been the target of quite a few novel approaches.

His revulsion to the idea she'd come here on the make was strong. He didn't want her to be like that. Yet she *was* sizing up the men in the gallery. And dismissing them, one by one.

Cynicism soured his mind as he continued to observe her meticulous assessment of the male half of the company. If he was her mark, he was in the mood to string her along for a while before delivering a comeuppance she wouldn't forget in a hurry. He despised freeloaders. He'd worked damned hard to get where he was. A pretty face and a beguiling body bought nothing from him. Except space in his bed if he really felt enticed to take what was offered.

She came through the archway that linked the two rooms on the first floor of the gallery. Jim tensed as her gaze swung towards him. Any second now, the moment of truth. He waited, a savage challenge brooding in his mind, his eyes simmering with dark intent.

She found him, her eyes widening as he stared straight at her. A questioning? An expectation of some response from him? Almost as if he should recognise her. Well, she was bound to disappointment if she thought that old line would work on him. He'd never seen her before in his life.

If there was one thing Jim prided himself on, it was total recall, people, places, figures. It was his one great talent, the means by which he had climbed to the pinnacle he now occupied, the hottest financier in town. The woman in yellow was not, and never had been, part of his world.

Her expression changed. It was as though she had mentally stepped back from her first reaction. She studied him with an intensity he found oddly discomforting. He could feel her trying to burrow under his skin to see the man inside. It was a cool, steady, calculating look, the kind an astute man might give in sizing up someone he was dealing with, not even a hint of sexuality in it.

It provoked Jim into moving, taking the initiative from her. She wanted to meet him? Fine! She would meet him on his terms.

He had a compelling urge to reduce her to simply another woman, a woman responding to him as a man. He wanted to strip off her deceptive cloak of spring, unmask both her body and mind. He wanted her flesh in his hands, naked of any illusion, grinding her into compliance to his will.

Deliberately he slid his eyes over the lush fullness of her breasts, his mouth curving into a smile of male appreciation. Her short skirt gave him a good view of her legs, too, long and lissome in silk stockings. He imagined them wound around him in submission. He would give her one hell of a serve for tricking him.

No one fooled Jim Neilson for long.

He was too wise in the ways of the world.

The yellow had been nothing but a spotlight. An impact colour. It would give him a lot of satisfaction... taking it off her.

CHAPTER TWO

HEAT flooded through Beth. She hadn't anticipated this—this sizing her up as a bed-worthy woman. He must have interpreted her staring at him as a come-on. Her stomach squirmed. Her mind whirled into a chaos of embarrassment.

To find him scrutinising her had been a heart-thumping shock. At first she'd thought... But he hadn't recognised her. Not so much as a glimmer of anything familiar to him. Then somehow, she hadn't been able to tear her eyes away. The pull was too strong to resist, to look for something left of the boy she had known.

Jamie, Jamie, her mind called to him, willing him to hear, to see, to remember. She had believed so strongly the bond between them would never be broken. Yet he hadn't come to her as he vowed he would.

Where did it go, the feeling they'd shared? What forces had severed it for him? She didn't understand. Never would. It had been too real to her. Even though she had been little more than a child when they'd parted, the certainty had been deep and abiding that they were meant to be together.

Eight years they had known each other, their understanding growing, deepening, a love that was more than love though they had never acknowledged it in words. It went beyond words. An intermingling of spirits or an intuitive communion of minds.

But there was nothing now. Nothing coming back from him except the kind of interest a man took in a woman he found attractive. Or were his instincts picking up something else, undefined yet tantalising enough to want to dig deeper?

He moved, coming straight at her, and she found it impossible to look away or turn aside. Her feet seemed rooted to the floor. Her pulse was drumming in her ears. Her mind couldn't come to grips with what she should do.

He was no longer the Jamie who had lived in her memory. Far from it. Fifteen years and an entirely different range of experience separated them from the childhood they'd shared in the valley. The last time she'd seen him in the flesh he was fifteen, she thirteen. And he was so different now. Not even the photographs had prepared her for this much difference.

His eyes locked onto hers, hard and compelling, sizzling with sexual signals. In some weird way it both frightened and excited her. No escape from a direct confrontation. He was not going to let her go easily. She was his quarry at the moment, and his concentration on her was like a magnetic force.

She could sense the dangerous, ruthless edge to him, the steely will of a survivor, a mind constantly watchful, determined on knowing, sifting, acting. It completely unnerved her. Yet she should have realised it had to be there in him to get where he was.

All the clippings Aunty Em had sent from newspapers and business magazines, reporting on the spectacular rise of Jim Neilson in financial circles, the man with the Supercray computer mind, the analytical genius, always one step ahead of market trends . . . It had surely been implicit in those columns if she'd been objective enough to read between the lines.

He was always referred to as Jim. Never Jamie. Never any mention of his earlier life. It was Aunty Em's opinion he had comprehensively blocked that out, and he wouldn't welcome any reminder of the past. It was behind him. Dead and deeply buried. If he'd wanted to reconnect with Beth or any of the Delaney family, he'd had more than enough years—and money—to do so.

She had accepted that long ago, yet she'd still been drawn to take this chance of having a look at the man he had become. More than look, if she was ruthlessly honest with herself. The need to know, finally and conclusively, had to be laid to rest.

Suddenly challenged with meeting him face to face, she frantically fretted over what to say. He might hate her for bringing his valley life back to him. Might also put all sorts of false interpretations on her coming here to see him, now that he was regarded as someone worth knowing.

She inwardly recoiled from such an outcome. *Let it go,* her mind screamed, even as he spoke and forced her to meet the immediate present.

"Can I offer you a glass of champagne?"

Her throat was dry. "Yes. Thank you," she managed to say huskily. He was so close to her. Couldn't he see Beth in her eyes?

He smiled as he handed the glass to her, a winning smile designed to charm a woman he was meeting for the first time. "You have the advantage over me."

His voice had deepened since he was fifteen. His tone was low, sexy, seductive. It had a mesmerising effect on her. She didn't catch his meaning. "Pardon?"

"You know who I am," he stated, his eyes subtly challenging her to deny it.

"Yes," she admitted. Stupid to pretend otherwise. Her smile was wry. "I know many things about you. But that's not really knowing you, is it?"

He laughed. It was a dark sound. Her skin prickled, instinct warning her to beware. This was not Jamie. This was very much a predatory male on the prowl.

"Media reports on me are usually slanted to suit the journalist," he said mockingly. "Much better to do your own personal research."

Blatant suggestiveness. Beth tried to push aside the disturbing physical element to satisfy some of her curiosity about him. "Do you ever let anyone into your private world?"

"I've just opened my door to you. Would you like to progress to, shall we say, a more intimate level?"

The sexual magnetism he was projecting took her breath away. Almost everything about him took her breath away. He was a head taller than she was, and she was above average height. His once slight and wiry physique was now solid with hard muscle, exuding masculinity.

His face no longer had a lean and hungry look. It was filled out in a strikingly handsome way, strong and firm, aggressively male, the brilliant intelligence in his dark eyes adding a dynamic quality that made it difficult to look away from him. His thick black hair was closely cropped, like a shiny helmet, emphasising a sleek animal appeal that was highlighted by his black leather jacket.

Beth found herself wondering whether his expertise as a lover would live up to the pulse-quickening promise of his looks. He was arrogantly confident of his attraction. No doubt he had every reason to be. But what did he deliver when it came to intimacy?

She sipped the champagne, giving her heart time to calm down while she considered how best to handle what was happening. It was totally outside any scenario she had imagined.

"Come now, don't go shy on me," he chided. "I much prefer spontaneity to calculation."

Hard cynicism behind his surface amusement. The impulse to probe a little spurred her to ask,

"Do you make a habit of picking up women on a whim?"

"No. I tend to be very selective. Consider yourself an exception to the rule."

The hope that wouldn't be stifled kicked through her heart. "Why make an exception of me?" Did he feel something? A faint thread of familiarity teasing his mind?

"I was bored with women in black. Your yellow suit caught my eye. Then you caught my eye. Are you going to tell me your name?"

She shook her head, knowing it would bring an abrupt end to this strangely piquant encounter. To tell him would shame her. If he didn't feel it...

"What point is there in remaining a mystery woman?" His eyes narrowed. "Are you married?"

"No."

"Attached?"

"No."

She thought of Gerald and felt only relief that she had ended their relationship. She'd found his academic world too constricting in the end, and Gerald too full of himself and his life to see anything else. Besides, meeting Jim Neilson was an object lesson to her. Even if nothing came of it, the sheer physical stimulation he generated showed her what she'd been missing out on. Next time she wouldn't settle for anything less. If there was a next time.

Her left hand was suddenly grasped and lifted, strong, purposeful fingers running over hers, feeling for indentations. Her skin seemed to spring alive under the cursory touch. She quelled the impulse to snatch her hand away, a silly overreaction.

"Satisfied?" she asked, realising he'd been checking for rings and ring marks.

His eyes blazed into hers. "No. We've a long way to go before I'm satisfied, golden girl. Come and have dinner with me."

He didn't wait for a response. He set off, weaving through the crowd, pulling her after him, her hand firmly wrapped in his. Without staging a public scene, Beth had little option but to follow, her mind whirling over his arrogant assumption she would fall in with his wishes, her heart fluttering at the thought of being alone with him. A flash came to her of Jamie pulling her after him up the bush track to the old quarry, saying she was safe with him. He'd look after her.

But this wasn't Jamie.

Confusion roared through her in turbulent waves. She felt she was being tugged in all sorts of directions—memories, needs that had never been answered, dreams that were suddenly all awry and permeating everything, an acute awareness of the strength of the hand, the strength of the man who was making her follow him, his powerful aura of decision, action, command holding her more captive than the fingers clamped around her wrist.

They reached the steps leading to the entrance of the gallery. Jim Neilson paused to hand his glass to the attendant who'd let Beth in. "Nice showing," he said. "Mind taking care of these for us?"

"My pleasure, Mr. Neilson," came the obliging reply, the attendant swiftly relieving Beth of her glass, as well. "See anything you like?" A hopeful inquiry.

"Another time." The dismissal discouraged further conversation.

Jim Neilson was already on the move again, sweeping Beth down the steps to the door. He hustled her out to the dark, tree-lined street, then adjusted his pace to a side-by-side stroll, his hand still firmly possessing hers. They were effectively alone together.

Beth struggled with a sense of disbelief. She and Jamie after all these years. Except he didn't know who she was. Didn't care. It was crazy to go along with this virtual abduction. There was not the slightest possibility of reviving their old relationship. He was different. He made her feel different. She should ask him to let her go.

She glanced at their hands, feeling the physical link tingling up to her brain and down to her toes. What did he want satisfied? Maybe he did feel something.

Beth was acutely conscious of never having felt satisfied herself. The bond with Jamie had spoiled any chance of a sense of rightness with anyone else. She'd tried with Gerald, tried to fool herself it was good enough. Had Jim Neilson found satisfaction with the women there must have been in his life?

He certainly wouldn't have been celibate all these years. What would it be like to feel all of him touching all of her? It was madness to be even thinking about it. Yet she wanted to know. This was the man Jamie had become. Long, powerful legs. Her gaze travelled to the broad shoulders that needed no padding to make them look as though he could easily heft her over one of them and carry her off.

Her heart skipped into a faster beat. Effectively he was doing that right now. She lifted her gaze to his face, wishing she could read his mind. The shadows of the night frustrated her. She could trace Jamie in his profile, the resolute set of his mouth and the determined jut of his chin. He'd been a fighter, never lacking the courage to stand up for himself, a proud boy, driven through the crucible of his grandfather's cruel meanness. What else had he survived to forge the dominance he'd achieved in his present world?

So much she wanted to know.

"Where are you taking me?" Her voice came out thin and wispy, reflecting her feeling that she was caught in two time frames, lost and treading uncertain ground.

A brief glance, a glitter in his eyes that ignited the sense of danger. Madness to feel so drawn to him in a situation that reeked of potential damage. To both of them. This meeting couldn't lead to any fruitful future. Their paths would inevitably diverge.

"My car is parked a couple of blocks away," he answered. "It's not far to walk."

His car. Part of his new life. "What make is it?" she asked, still riding the temptation to learn more about him.

A sardonic smile. "Didn't your research pick that up?"

She frowned, jolted by the cynical tone in his voice. Her admission of knowing who he was must have prompted an assumption she knew more than she did. Research suggested he thought she was a journalist. Or worse, a gold-digger out to latch onto a wealthy meal ticket.

Should she correct him? But what could she say? How to explain her interest without revealing the truth?

The irony was, her so-called research consisted of a few articles and a couple of mentions in social columns, including an abbreviated guest list for tonight's exhibition. It wasn't enough. Not nearly enough. Having dinner with him would tell her much more. He'd set this ball rolling. She didn't want to stop it. Not yet.

"It's a Porsche." Another glittering glance. "Satisfied?"

A sexy sports model, sleek, powerful, capable of devouring whatever road he chose to take,

driving past everyone else. Probably black, too.
"It fits," she said, more to herself than to him.

"I'm glad you're not disappointed," he said
dryly.

She was, deep down. Disappointed he hadn't
recognised her, though she couldn't really have
expected it on a superficial level. Even at thirteen,
her hair had only slightly yellowed from the
snowy white it had been through most of her
childhood. It was almost brown now. She'd done
a lot of growing up since Jamie had last seen her.
A late bloomer, her mother had often said.

Having seen recent photographs of him, it was
easier for her to identify the boy in the man, despite the changes. Still, when he had looked into
her eyes... Surely they were the same, almond-
shaped and deeply lidded, their amber irises quite
an unusual and distinctive colour.

Golden girl. The name he'd given her brought
a wry smile. He'd once said she was the only gold
in his life. Why hadn't the bond between them
lasted?

She shook her head. Obviously it had meant
more to her than to him. As Aunty Em said, he'd
had the means to come to her if he'd wanted to.
He'd picked her up tonight by chance, a stranger,
to relieve his boredom. Or was it more than that?
Did he feel the underlying tug of another time
and place, an attraction he was pursuing beyond
any rational thought?

She moved her fingers over the knuckles of his,
wishing she was a clairvoyant who could see the

future through the power of touch. His skin was warm, despite the coolness of the September evening. How did he transmit the electric vibrancy that was racing through her?

They turned a corner. Another narrow, tree-lined street, terrace houses crowding the sidewalk, their porches trimmed with ornate iron-lace fences. An old area of Sydney, Woollhara. It was close to the city centre and the harbour, newly fashionable again, the houses expensively renovated to suit the taste of wealthy people. She'd walked around here this afternoon, casing the area, dithering over whether to attempt gate-crashing the private showing in the gallery or leave well enough alone.

Who'd have thought she'd be walking hand in hand with Jamie—Jim—a few hours later? A burst of light-headed laughter bubbled forth.

"What's funny?" he asked.

She grinned at him, dizzy with her daring. "I can't believe I'm with you like this."

The flash of his eyes seared her with a sobering reminder this was no child's play between them. They were into a very adult game here. A quiver ran down her thighs. Should she stop now?

He stopped. He took a key ring from his jacket and released her hand to unlock the passenger door of the car at the kerb beside them. The distinctive lines of the Porsche gave her heart and mind a jolt. This was real. A black Porsche, low, dark, threatening. The old warning shrieked through her mind—never get in a car with a stranger.

Jim Neilson swung the door open for her.

If she stepped into that space... Why was she suddenly seeing it as a black hole, infinitely dangerous? The tension of decision held her momentarily paralysed.

"Not turning coward on me, are you?" he softly mocked.

She looked wildly at him, hearing Jamie daring her to be as brave as he was, her heart pounding madly, fear fighting with the need to earn Jamie's respect and admiration. Except this was Jim Neilson, and she was a stranger to him, so how could her compliance with his game earn respect or admiration?

"Believe this!" he said harshly, and in the next instant, before she could even draw breath, she was pinned to his chest, held imprisoned there by the unrelenting strength of an arm that denied her any attempt at resistance as he curled his other hand around her cheek and chin and forcibly tilted her face to the angle he wanted. His teeth flashed, white and wolfish. "An appetiser," he promised.

Beth barely had time to gasp. His mouth covered hers, invading it with shocking swiftness, no pause for persuasive or seductive preliminaries. His tongue embroiled hers in an erotic tangle, darting provocatively, sweeping her palate with sensational effect, inciting a fiercely primitive response. It was as though he'd pressed some dormant trigger in her, exploding a deeply buried mine of sexuality that demanded satisfaction.

A torrent of feelings pumped through her— anger to have waited so long to experience this, frustration that he'd never come for her, never invited her to share in his new life, a fierce jealousy of the women he had given himself to, a seething desire to take all he offered, experience it to the hilt, make him remember her for the rest of his life, whether he wanted to or not.

She clawed her fingers up his leather jacket, thrust them through the thick mat of his hair, curled them around his skull, urging on the passionate plunder that could not be called a kiss. Not from him. Not from her. A kiss was an exchange of good feelings, warm feelings, a wish to give and take pleasure. This was the boiling blood of a battlefield, each of them striving to win concessions from the other.

She sensed his drive for submission from her. She wouldn't give it. With sheer wanton provocation, she rubbed her lower body against his, feeding the frenzy of released feeling, exulting in the hard bulge of his erection, hating him for being so aroused by a woman he'd merely picked up. A nobody to him. Yet he could do this to her, with her, an intimacy that had no grounds for intimacy on his side. Just sheer animal lust, taking, uncaring of the object being taken.

It was obscene.

She wanted to kick him. She wanted to kill him. She wanted him to want her because she was Beth. Damn him! Damn him to hell for closing his door on her! Forgetting her!

"Feeling hungry?" he growled, his hands scooping her bottom and squeezing her into more aggressive contact, a blatant and unashamed pressure against her stomach.

"Yes," she hissed, uncaring what he thought.

He swung her around and lowered her onto the passenger seat of the Porsche, lifting her legs in with a smooth economy of movement. "Then let's get to the feast," he said, his eyes challenging her appetite for it as he stood back and closed the door.

One night, she thought fiercely. One night to make up for what she had missed. One night to take all she might have had if circumstances had been different. She felt cheated, bereft, pumped up with wild and perilous purpose.

He sank onto the seat beside her, closed his door, started the engine with a roar. "Fasten your seat belt," he rasped.

"You're right," she snapped, whipping the belt across her body and clicking it into place. Her eyes clashed with his in fiery challenge. "It could be a bumpy ride."

He revved the motor, his foot playing with the accelerator as he assessed the glitter in her no-holds-barred gaze. "You pack one hell of a punch, golden girl," he said, then turned his attention to getting the Porsche on the road.

They took off into the night.

The tension in the car jangled every nerve in Beth's body.

She didn't care.

She didn't care where they went or what they did.

She was going to see this night through with Jim Neilson.

Then, maybe, she could bury Jamie once and for all.

CHAPTER THREE

"TAKE off your jacket."

The casual command kicked another burst of adrenaline through Beth. She bit down on a blistering retort and gave him a veiled look that hid lethal thoughts.

He leaned indolently against the side wall of the private elevator he'd just activated, assessing her with hot, lustful eyes. They were zooming to the top level of some tall building at Circular Quay. Beth didn't have to be told he wasn't taking her to a restaurant. He wanted control. Absolute control.

She shifted her stance, relaxing against the wall facing him, her eyes simmering with the need to strip him naked. In every sense. "Take yours off," she commanded.

A quirky little smile gave his mouth a more sensual curve as he pushed forward enough to shrug his shoulders out of the jacket and drag it off his arms. "Leather doesn't turn you on?"

"I prefer the touch of human skin."

"Then I'd better get rid of my shirt, too."

The jacket was dropped on the floor. She watched his hands start on his shirt buttons, his fingers nimbly making short work of opening up

the black silk, revealing a tantalising arrow of
black hair zeroing down to his jeans.

"You're lagging behind," he taunted, his gaze
fastened pointedly on her breasts.

Beth slid off the shoulder strap of her handbag
and let it fall. She smiled as she thought of the
sexy lingerie she was wearing, a gift from her
younger sister Kate, along with the advice it was
well past time for Beth to get herself a red-hot
lover. Kate had not been enamoured with Gerald.
No doubt she would think Jim Neilson fitted the
bill.

His shoulders needed no padding. There was
nothing weedy about his arms, either. His skin
gleamed like polished bronze over tightly packed
muscle. He had a torso that would draw admiring stares from both men and women. The
thought of touching him, running her hands over
his magnificently delineated chest, was so attractive, Beth told herself clawing would be more
in order. She drew off her jacket, and defiantly
matching his carelessness, tossed it on top of his
clothes.

"Very saucy," he commented, his gaze sizzling
over the provocative swirl of black lace, cun-
ningly designed to focus the eye on the flesh-
coloured fabric stretching over her aureoles.

Beth felt her nipples tighten.

"Delectable." The throaty murmur reflected
his arousal as he suddenly crowded the space between them, taking her hands, lifting them above

her head, pinning them to the wall with such swift action Beth was caught by surprise.

The elevator stopped.

The doors opened.

His eyes mocked her distraction. Nothing deterred him from bending his head to her upraised breasts, tugging her nipples to more distended prominence with his teeth, sucking on them with stomach-curling power, leaving the thin fabric of her bra hot and wet and totally transparent. It was so incredibly erotic, Beth held her breath and let it happen, fascinated by the movement of his mouth, enthralled by the sensations arcing from it.

She didn't want him to stop, but he did, straightening and sliding her arms down the wall to her sides as he stared at the effect he'd had on her, smiling in satisfaction at the dark, hardened nubs. His eyes flicked to hers, black, brilliant, piercing in their intensity.

"Was the entree to your liking?"

Beth swallowed, collected her scattered wits and answered, "I hope the main course lives up to it."

He laughed and bent to scoop up their clothes. "I wouldn't rob you of the right setting." He nodded to the opened passage out of the elevator. "Go ahead. Enter my private world. I'll show you everything I have."

Beth willed strength into her quivery legs and preceded him out of the elevator, straight-shouldered, maintaining an air of dignity despite her state of exposure, heart thundering in anticipation of his next move, mind set on holding her own throughout this encounter with Jim Neilson.

He switched on ceiling spotlights as she stepped from a tiled foyer to a carpeted living room. Her high heels sank into the thick, dove-grey pile. She paused to take off her shoes and drink in Jim Neilson's habitat. It had the obvious luxury of spaciousness and the stark impact of almost characterless modernism.

The furnishings looked clinical—chrome, glass, black leather, a grey vertical blind blocking out the end wall, which was undoubtedly glass for what had to be a spectacular view from this high up. The chairs and sofas and tables were certainly functional, probably state-of-the-art in their styling, but they seemed more like show-pieces than home pieces.

A disturbing Brett Whitely painting seemed to leap off the wall facing her, strident in its lines and colour. She was staring at it, feeling it was like some nightmare she wouldn't like to live with, when she felt hands at her waist, the release of the button at the back of her skirt, the zipper drawn down. A gentle pull over her hips and the garment circled her feet.

For a moment, all she could think of was how much more exposed she was, the sexy lace panties reduced to little more than a G-string slicing between her buttocks, the garter belt holding up her stockings offering no better protection. Then

warm palms slid down to cup the soft, naked
roundness of her bottom, fingers splaying over
it.

Her heart leapt into her mouth. She had to do
something and do it fast. No way was she going
to be Jim Neilson's sexual victim. She wouldn't
let him think it, either. He was *her* chosen lover
for the night.

She sucked in a deep breath and swung around,
her fingers digging into the waistband of his
jeans, her mouth homing in on his nipples as she
ripped the stud apart and tore his zipper down.
The art of surprise wasn't all his, she thought
savagely, feeling his stomach contract, his chest
expand.

She tugged and licked at the relatively small
protusions of flesh, exulting in his hardening reaction to the stimulation. She pushed his jeans
and underpants down his loins, extracted the taut,
hefty piston of his manhood, weighing it deliberately in her hand as she drew back to look at it,
a mad boldness seizing her mind.

"The equipment is first class," she mocked,
rubbing her thumb over its moist tip, stroking
her fingers along its full length before dismissing
it, turning away to sashay to the blind at the end
of the room. "I also like to take in every view,"
she added silkily, finding the cords that operated
the slats and yanking them to sweep the blind to
the other side of the window.

A stunning panorama of the harbour gleamed
at her, the huge coat hanger bridge looming

beyond the busy ferry terminal at Circular Quay, the magnificent sails that roofed the Opera House curving brightly into the night sky, the massed foreshore lights of the northern suburbs winking like thousands of fireflies. The realisation hit her that she was standing in what had to be a million-dollar penthouse apartment. And the owner of such prime real estate was used to having whatever he wanted.

She heard the thud of shoes landing on the carpet, the swoosh of clothes being discarded, the soft pad of footsteps, the crackle of paper being torn. Paper? No, a packet of some sort. He probably carried condoms in his wallet. He'd be mad not to practise safe sex in a situation like this. She'd be mad, too.

She was probably certifiably insane as it was, but normal rules didn't apply to this night. It was time out of time, and there was a fever in her blood that demanded a sense of completion, come what may.

Her skin prickled with anticipation. The next move was his. She adopted a relaxed stance and ignored his presence behind her, fixing her gaze on the harbour traffic far below. She didn't care that he could view her naked backside at leisure. In some perverse way she enjoyed flaunting it at him. It excited her, thinking of him looking at her, planning what he would do next, sizzling with the need to reduce her to his plaything again.

Fingertips grazing over the backs of her knees. It was an act of will to remain absolutely still.

The tantalising touch sliding up her thighs, muscles tensing. The suspenders of her garter belt unclipped, back and front, fingers trailing up the lacy leg edge of her panties, flesh crawling with sensitivity, belt removed and tossed away, a nail-thin caress up the curve of her spine, raising an uncontrollable, convulsive shiver, bra unfastened, thumbs hooking under the shoulder straps, drawing them down her arms, letting them fall, a soft, silky rolling down of her stockings, ankles and feet tantalisingly caressed as he lifted each one in turn.

It was the most erotic undressing Beth had ever experienced. It electrified both her body and her mind to an acute awareness.

She could feel his breath, sense his heat even before he positioned his body against hers, the hard roll of his erection sliding up towards the pit of her back, his arms encircling her waist, palms pushing up over her nipples and subjecting them to a teasing, rotating motion that had every muscle in her body clenching.

"You seem quite transfixed by the view." The mocking murmur was close to her ear.

Beth fought to remain clear-headed over the turmoil he was wreaking in her body. "Do you enjoy it or is it simply a status symbol to you?" she asked, reaching back to draw her fingernails over the rock-hard muscles of his thighs, wishing she could dig under his skin.

"I like climbing mountains," he answered. "Getting to the peak."

The sexual allusion to what he was doing to her was not lost on Beth, yet she sensed he spoke the truth about himself. Jamie must have climbed a hundred mountains on his way to becoming this man. She wondered if he saw this apartment as a place where he was finally unassailable from ever being dragged down again.

He cupped her breasts, possessing them fully for a moment before sliding his hands over her stomach, burrowing under the flimsy lace that still covered her most private part.

"But valleys have their points of interest, too," he said, and with an expertise that was shockingly exciting, he parted her hidden cleft to a more accessible opening and began a stroking that aroused almost unbearably exquisite sensations.

She felt like hot putty melting under his touch. Her legs started to tremble. Desperate to maintain some self-control, Beth clutched at another question that had flitted through her mind. "Why did you choose the Brett Whitely painting?"

It distracted him momentarily, giving her a breather from the sweet torture. "It's a scream of the soul," he answered darkly and resumed his tactile concentration on the valley as he expounded further. "It's in every one of us, golden girl. You feel it, too... the scream for all that's unattainable.'

Yes. It was the scream that had brought her here with him. But what did he dream of? What did he crave? What was he missing in his life, this brave, new world he had conquered?

"That's why you're here, wanting this," he went on, his voice a drum in her ears.

No. She wanted more than this, she thought. The unattainable. And sadness for what could never be with the Jamie who was lost to her surged into her heart, drowning it, even as her flesh cried out for its intense excitement to be appeased.

The low beat of his voice continued. "No matter what we do, how we live, what we have, most of the time we hide from our souls, repress the truth, pretend..." His finger teasing the rim of her vagina, slowly working inwards, her muscles convulsing. "But deep inside, deep inside, golden girl...we scream."

The last word was hissed, loaded with sexual innuendo, and it was true of her physically—she *was* screaming for the fill of his flesh to ease the need he had incited. Yet her mind was floating above it, listening to the man he was revealing and revelling more in that intimacy than the other.

"You were going to show me everything," she reminded him.

His touch stilled. He withdrew it to remove her last piece of clothing. "Let me take you on a tour," he said, grasping her hand, drawing her into stepping out of her panties.

She had to force her tremulous legs to work, to follow him. His stimulation had left her feeling

liquified, uncoordinated, aching for far more
than he had given. Yet to concede any weakness
would feed his satisfaction at the cost of hers.
Keep him guessing, keep him working at getting
the subjugation to his will that he obviously
wanted, keep digging for what she wanted.

"Now on the opposite wall to the Brett Whitely
is an Arthur Boyd," he instructed, smiling
indulgently.

His nonchalant air was an act of will. A quick
glance showed his arousal had in no way abated.
It also gave Beth the reassurance he was sheathed
with protection. No risk of any unwelcome
consequences from this one-night stand. Which
was all it could be for both of them.

Again the sadness weighed heavily.

A meeting...a farewell.

"Stand here for the best view," he directed,
positioning her behind one of the black leather
sofas directly across the room from the painting.

It was a high-backed lounge. She automatically rested her hands on it, needing the support
of some solidity. He moved to her rear, as before,
talking over her shoulder.

"The subject matter looks so simple, but the
more you study this painting, the more you see
in it."

The colours were mostly dark greens and blues,
a night scene, a small house on the top of a hill,
below it a miniature white cow, seemingly
heading down to a lake. She saw nothing else in
the huge, sombre sweep of landscape. A white

crescent moon—no stars—formed a tiny white
curve in the sky.

Isolation, she thought. The painting brooded
with isolation, little objects starkly overwhelmed
by their much larger environment.

"There are hidden depths to it," he murmured, sliding a hand around her hip, over her
stomach. "Keep looking, golden girl. I want you
to see them...." He bent, his arm pulling her to
him, a knee parting her legs, a swift, smooth
guidance and he was inside her, plunging hard
and fast. "And feel them," he said with
throbbing satisfaction.

Beth clutched the sofa, instinctively anchoring
herself as she gasped, yet almost instantly she was
enthralled with the incredible feeling of him invading the passage he'd already prepared,
soothing the frustrated nerve ends and filling the
empty ache with the solid insertion of his
manhood—big, strong, pulsing with power. It
was marvellous, mind-blowing, body-shattering.

"Concentrate on the lake," he advised, rhyth-
mically setting her on a sea of sensation. "The
reflections..."

So strange to view the dark picture of isolation
while feeling the most intimate joining between
a man and a woman. The lake was still, not the
slightest shimmer of movement in its reflections.
Inside her the rushing flow and ebb of a tide that
crashed and swirled and sucked, a storming of
shores that welcomed the pounding, loved it,
revelled in it.

She wanted to let it flow through her, an experience to be savoured to the full. But there was still the compulsion to turn the tide on him, to reach for his innermost core, the heart and mind of the man who had once been Jamie. She forced herself to concentrate, to catch him while his guard was down, believing he'd taken all initiative from her.

"Does this painting..." Her voice was little more than a husky croak. She swallowed hard. "Reflect what you feel?" She pushed the words out, determined to commune with him on more than a physical level.

He buried himself as deeply as he could in her, paused. "What do you imagine I feel?" A raw edge to his voice.

She drew on her knowledge of Jamie. Was he still inside the man she held in such intimate possession? "The white cow, a lonely outcast, a long, cold night... Did you have a need for me?"

"Hardly an outcast." Harsh. A slow withdrawal as he made a sardonic point. "When one is wanted by so many. And so much..." He rammed home his full length and paused again. "Even by a woman who's only read about me."

But he was wrong about her, and he sensed it somehow. There was a wondering note in his tone. She seized on the hint of vulnerability, riding the moment as hard as he was riding her, mental against physical.

"I think you want a full moon." She rushed the words out, fiercely gathering her thoughts against the active chaos he stirred. "But what is pictured...is a thin crescent...a partial...and it will never grow into anything else." She closed her eyes, swept up in the maelstrom of feeling, fighting the tide to put the last critical question. "Is that what makes you scream?"

"A full moon for lovers? Dream on, golden girl," he said derisively and drummed any coherent thought out of her mind with a wild vigour that smashed every last thread of control, both hers and his, climaxing with explosive force and leaving them panting in paroxysms of intense release.

Spent, shuddering in reaction, he wrapped her in his arms and clamped her against him, their naked bodies slick with heat and almost excruciatingly sensitive to touch.

"Is my skin hot enough for you?" he growled. "I wouldn't want you to feel cold...or lonely."

She didn't speak. Her head was spinning, her body churning with the knowledge of how it felt to be taken so comprehensively, as though she was branded inside and out by his possession.

"Maybe we should move to another painting," he taunted. "Or have you been shown as much as you want?"

She hesitated. He had seized and still held a dominating position. And was arrogantly confident of keeping it. If she stayed, undoubtedly she would be committing herself to a night of saturation sex. But knowledge came in many forms. And touch—as he had just shown her—could reach many places.

"I'm not satisfied yet," she answered resolutely.

And probably never will be, came the hollow thought. But the night was still young. He wouldn't back down from the challenge implicit in her words, not a man who had to climb mountains and stand on top of them. If she could only touch him beyond the physical. She had barely scratched the surface of the inner man.

Jim Neilson was well and truly in the ring right now.

Would Jamie emerge before it was over?

CHAPTER FOUR

BETH stood under the shower in the guest bathroom of Jim Neilson's penthouse apartment, trying to soothe aching muscles and revive herself for the long day ahead. Her mind dredged up the consoling thought that it hadn't been a totally fruitless night. At least she'd had the experience of a red-hot lover once in her lifetime. Though she suspected the memory would be soured by the failure of her real quest.

Heaving a deep sigh that expressed frustration and resignation, she turned off the taps. No point in looking back any more. The man she'd left asleep in his bed was so encased in self-made armour, he was not about to let anyone break it open. Her probing had been turned away again and again. If Jamie still existed somewhere, he was suppressed under so many layers he was unreachable.

Despondently she towelled herself dry, then sorted through the clothes she'd collected from the living room. Her yellow suit was hopelessly crumpled. Not that it mattered how she looked this morning. She was not about to meet anyone she knew. Once she was at her hotel, she would have plenty of time to change into a fresh outfit before Aunty Em collected her for their trip to the old farm.

Nevertheless, she didn't feel comfortable in the clothes that had been stripped off her by Jim Neilson. She knew she would never wear them again. Needs must, until she could get to her luggage.

Grimacing at her reflection in the bathroom mirror, she reached for her handbag, took out a hairbrush and lipstick and proceeded to achieve a fairly respectable appearance. Having braced herself to get on with her life, she left the bathroom and headed down the hallway, hoping the private elevator would not present any problem in making a quick and quiet getaway.

Wrapped in her own purpose, she was several steps into the living room before the aroma of freshly brewed coffee registered. Her feet faltered as she frowned at the smell. It had to mean . . .

"Good morning."

Her heart lurched. Her head jerked around to face the source of the unexpected and unwelcome greeting. He stood by the huge picture window she had unveiled last night, a steaming mug of coffee in his hand. Although a black silk robe covered him from shoulder to knee, it did not diminish the impact of powerful virility. Instead it increased his sexual appeal, the belt loosely looped, ready to fall open with a finger flick, the deep V neckline showing an inviting expanse of raw masculinity.

Beth felt her throat drying up. There wasn't one inch of his body she wasn't intimately acquainted with, and it was a magnificent male body. But in the end, it was just a body, she fiercely reminded herself.

He showed no surprise that she was dressed. He waved casually to the long glass table between the sofas where he'd set down a tray—coffee, milk, sugar, biscuits. "I'd hate you to go without some sustenance," he said with one of his quirky smiles.

"Why?" she asked bluntly, ignoring the tug of physical attraction.

He shrugged. "Perhaps I want to show you I can be civilised."

"You've shown me all your sides. I don't need to be shown any more."

He raised a mocking eyebrow. "Giving up?"

Her smile was wry. "I know when I'm beaten."

"Perhaps not." There was a curious expression in his eyes. "Give me your name."

She shook her head. "It's irrelevant. This is goodbye."

He frowned. "What if I don't want it to be goodbye?"

"It is, anyway."

"It was great sex," he reminded her with wicked appeal.

"Yes," she conceded flatly. *Though ultimately soul-destroying*, she added, crushing the wistful thought that it might have been different if he'd opened the doors she'd knocked on.

"What more do you want?" he pressed, looking for a response he could work on.

The doors to Jamie were locked. Beth had come to the conclusion that Jim Neilson had thrown away the keys and that what she wanted was irretrievable. Not even the greatest sex in the world could make up for it. It only made the loss greater.

"I want to go now," she said decisively. "I have other things to do."

He turned to face her full on. She felt the unleashed blast of his formidable concentration as his eyes probed hers with all their brilliant and magnetic intensity. "Not once have you used my name," he said with slow deliberation. "Now you're going without telling me yours. Did you intend all along for us to be ships passing in the night?"

She shrugged, dismissing the point as of no real importance. "It was always a possibility."

He nodded consideringly. "You turned last night into a contest."

"Did I?" She paused, her eyes mocking his view of what had happened between them. "Or did you?" She threw the question at him.

His mouth twisted. "Why do I have the feeling there is more to this encounter than you're letting on?"

"Why worry?" she asked him flippantly. "You won the contest. You didn't let me get to you. You stayed on top."

"If you go, I lose," he stated with a certainty that puzzled her.

"I'm sure you can generate great sex with any amount of women," she said sceptically.

"No. It was the mental fight. Something...quite different." He hesitated, seemingly feeling his way along uncharted territory. "I think I've been looking for someone like you for a very long time."

The sickening irony of those words cut deep. "No, you haven't," she retorted with blistering certainty.

"Shouldn't I be the judge of that?"

"If you'd been really looking, you'd have found me long before this."

His eyes narrowed on the burning derision in hers. "Perhaps I've been blind."

"No." The bitterness of total defeat poured into words before she could stop them. "You've been too busy being Jim Neilson. I think you'll never be anyone else but Jim Neilson now. So I'm leaving, because I didn't come for Jim Neilson and I don't belong in Jim Neilson's life. Is that enough recognition of your name for you?"

"For whom did you come?" he asked her, homing in instantly on the one significant point.

She sighed, wrung out by this futile confrontation. She looked at him with dull, weary eyes, seeing the aggressive vitality of the conqueror determined on climbing another mountain. But her mountain had been climbed, and she was returning to the valley he'd put behind him.

"Who *are* you?" he demanded, propelled from his stance at the window of his private eyrie, high in the sky above the city he'd made his. He came straight for her, unprepared to let her go when *he* wasn't satisfied.

The urge to hit him in the face with it was strong. Her deep disappointment, the long years of wondering and the final frustration of last night's intense campaign to reach him—all surged together in a compelling need for some kind of recognition from him, a glimmer of memory...even if he hated it.

"I'm Beth Delaney." She shot the words at him.

It stopped him dead in his tracks. Shock, confusion, a wild searching for features that would confirm her identity to him, a glassy stare at her eyes, recoil, then slowly the dawning of realisation, a look of appalled horror at her re-emergence in his life and the form it had taken.

It gave Beth savage satisfaction to see he hadn't completely forgotten her. The years they had shared were not a blank to him, either. Though Aunty Em was right. He didn't like having them recalled. But be damned if she would let him off scot-free now. He'd forced the issue. She proceeded to give him the answers he'd demanded, straight between the eyes.

"I came looking for Jamie."

His chin jutted. A muscle in his cheek flinched.

"He once said he would come to me when he could."

His throat moved convulsively.

"He never did. Not once in fifteen years."

No glitter in his eyes now, only dark turbulence.

"Last night I had the chance to look him up. But Jamie was gone. I only found Jim Neilson."

His mouth thinned into a grim line.

"Now it's time for Beth Delaney to go, too," she said with bleak finality. "There's nothing left of what there once was. I guessed it had to be so, but I wanted to see for myself. That's all."

She turned and headed for the tiled foyer. There was nothing to hold her here. No doubt Jim Neilson would only feel intense relief at seeing her go, a ghost from the past he didn't want to remember.

"Wait!"

The snapped command fell like a whiplash across her shoulders. It was totally unexpected, cutting through her suppositions, heart-jolting in its seeming senselessness. She gathered herself to look at him once more, turning her head but not her feet. They were set on her own path.

He hadn't moved. Tension seemed to have stretched the skin on his face tighter, highlighting its strongly boned lines. His hands were clenched at his sides. Fighting himself, Beth thought. His dark eyes looked like burning coals from hell.

"Where did you come from?" he asked.

"Melbourne. You might recall it was where my family moved after the bank sold up our farm," she added sardonically.

It didn't score a hit. He'd already donned his armour against recollections of the past.

"Are you going back to Melbourne?" A searching missile, targeted at a danger point to him.

"That's up in the air. Though don't let it concern you. I won't intrude on your life again. Jim Neilson is absolutely safe from me."

Her assurance was ignored. "Where are you going to from here? Today." His mind was on one track. Self-protection.

She heaved an exasperated sigh. "Nowhere you want to know. I'm going back to the valley. Our old family farm is up for auction this afternoon. If I can buy it, I will. For my father. As strange as it might seem to you, he left his heart there." Her smile was self-mocking. "Maybe I did, too."

He said nothing, just stared at her as though she was a nightmare he wished he'd never dreamed.

"Goodbye, Jim Neilson," she said firmly, and walked to the elevator, her high heels clacking hollow echoes on the tiled floor of the foyer.

There was no problem in effecting an exit. The elevator was waiting. She stepped into the private compartment and pressed the Down button. The tops of mountains were lonely places, she thought, wondering how much Jim Neilson valued his isolation, how much he liked it.

But that was none of her business.

The elevator doors closed.

Her brief encounter with him was closed.

She was going down...to the old valley where generations of her family had once lived. Back to her roots. Though she knew there would always be a ghost there for her. Impossible not to remember Jamie...in the valley.

CHAPTER FIVE

BETH.

The scream inside him demanded he follow, catch her, keep her. It took all his willpower to resist the irrational impulse, to shut the scream off, to tell himself what was broken was beyond mending.

He wasn't Jamie any more.

And she wasn't the Beth he'd idealised.

Maybe she never had been.

In a life of black and grey she had been colour, and he'd coloured a perfect dream with her at the centre of it. His Beth. But she hadn't lived up to it. There was no way past that. However wrong it was to feel a sense of betrayal, it still cut deeply. He couldn't bear to be with her.

With a groan of anguish for the way he'd taken her last night, he twisted away from the memory of her accusing figure and went to the window, staring at the far horizon, wondering how he was going to erase everything he'd done with her from his mind.

Bitter irony that she'd drawn his attention with colour, wearing yellow. Though it had been more than that, much more in the end. She'd got under his skin well and truly. No other woman had ever done that.

Beth. Knowing him from the past, using it... what for?

Why had she looked him up now?

The farm.

If I can buy it, she'd said.

She wasn't sure if she had enough finance.

That must be it.

He recoiled from the thought of going to the valley where the memories would spring alive again, yet the Delaney farm had once been his one haven of happiness. Beth's family had been good to him. They'd made him feel like one of them. It had got him through those years.

No, *she* had. He'd only ever seen the family as part of her. His fault—his circumstances, probably—that he'd built up that special bond in his mind. It hadn't meant the same to her.

He felt the scream lurking and savagely repressed it.

There was a debt to be paid, the only real debt he had. Now that he'd been reminded of it, he couldn't ignore it. Going to the auction would mean seeing her again, but he could steel himself to do it... one more time.

CHAPTER SIX

BETH found the ankle-length circular skirt and long-sleeved shirt of her sage green outfit comforting to wear. No exposure at all. The colour suited her mood, as well. She didn't feel bright this morning. Though she forced her spirits to lighten as she saw her aunt's car pull up outside the entrance to the hotel. After all, going to bid at an auction for former family property was an exciting venture.

Aunty Em would certainly sense something wrong if Beth did not respond appropriately. Her father's sister was a keenly perceptive woman. Not much got past her. Probably having five children had kept her on her toes, watchful for mischief and trouble.

"Only took me five minutes to get here," she declared cheerfully as Beth stepped into the passenger seat.

It prompted a smile. Since the Ramada Hotel was handily situated to where her aunt lived in the Sydney suburb of Ryde, a five-minute trip was about right. Beth glanced at her watch. "It's only just gone ten o'clock. You made good time."

"I do love this little car. It gets me around everywhere. And no trouble parking."

It was a bright purple Mazda 121, commonly called a bubble car, and unexpectedly roomy inside for its size. Which was just as well, since Aunty Em was a big woman—well cushioned for comfort, she always said—though not so big now as she used to be. The heart operation had forced her to lose weight, but it hadn't put a complete halt to her passion for cakes.

"I made a lovely moist orange cake for our picnic," she said in her next breath. "Chocolate icing."

"Sounds yummy. You're a great cook, Aunty Em."

She nodded happily and set the car in motion. "I'm really looking forward to seeing the old place again. I was brought up on that farm, you know."

Beth knew. Three generations of Delaneys had been brought up there. A lot of history and happiness and heartache. She looked fondly at her aunt, still as bouncy and full of life as she had always been, despite being almost sixty. Her hair was a grey frizz—reflecting a firm belief in permanent waves—and her full cheeks had dropped into jowls, but the cheerful smile and merry brown eyes kept old age at bay.

"It probably won't look the same after all this time," Beth warned kindly.

"Nothing's ever quite how we remember it," came the quick agreement, accompanied by a shrewd look. "Did you get to see Jamie last night?"

"I saw Jim Neilson." It was too bare a statement. She gave her aunt a rueful smile. "You're right. He's not the Jamie I remember. Very different."

"Did you introduce yourself to him?"

"It wasn't really appropriate."

She wished she'd kept her identity from him this morning, too. Stupid, vengeful impulse, achieving only hurt on both sides. Airing old wounds that should have been left alone. What satisfaction was there in it now? She tried to sigh away the tense turmoil still churning inside her from having given away so much of herself. For nothing.

"He didn't recognise me," she added flatly.

Her aunt sighed, too. "I'm sorry you were disappointed." A wealth of understanding in those few words.

Tears pricked Beth's eyes. She fiercely blinked them back. "I guess that's life," she said as lightly as she could.

"Yes. It keeps moving on. No matter what."

"It's lucky we've got a nice, sunny day. We'll be able to lay our picnic out near the creek."

Aunty Em was not slow to pick up the different conversational ball. The tender topic of Jamie was dropped. They were soon on the expressway north of Sydney, and it was only an hour to the exit that led to the valley they had once called home. They gradually fell silent as they drove into familiar territory, observing the changes that had taken place in the past fifteen years.

Turf farming had been introduced on the river flats. They passed a wholesale nursery for native plants and trees. Several properties carried commercial chicken sheds. At their gates were bags of poultry manure piled up for sale to passers-by. A horse stud specialised in showjumpers. Another advertised pony-club tuition.

They came to the beginning of the valley proper, and here a few of the old farms appeared more or less intact. The deeper they went into the valley, the less changes there were. Which was reassuring. There was no magic in returning to something that was radically different.

Surprisingly, the old schoolhouse looked functional, freshly painted, and the surrounding playground in good trim, obviously in use. Few one-teacher schools were operational these days. Children were mostly transported by bus to bigger school centres. Beth felt pleased that this community centre had survived the inroads of modern life.

The valley post office and general store remained opposite it, sentinels to the past. "I wonder if Mrs. Hutchens still rules behind the counter," she remarked.

Aunty Em chuckled. "Doris Hutchens. Biggest busybody I ever knew. Though she had most people's best interests at heart. Remember how she faced up to Jorgen Neilson and hauled Jamie off to school?"

"Yes."

The memory came flooding back. Jamie had been dumped on old Jorgen, the illegitimate son of his runaway daughter—who was no better than she should be, according to Mrs. Hutchens. No-one was quite sure of Jamie's age, but the figuring was he was old enough to be at school and Jorgen was holding him out to use as slave labour on his farm. In actual fact, he was seven when Doris Hutchens triumphantly presented him to the schoolmaster, and he had to suffer the ignominy of being placed in Beth's class of five-year-olds.

She had helped him learn to read and write. He'd learnt fast. He was much faster than her with numbers. It wasn't long before he zoomed past the schoolmaster in mathematics.

"Mean old tyrant, that Jorgen Neilson," Aunty Em muttered darkly. "He treated Jamie shamefully, you know. Made his home life a misery."

"Yes, I know," Beth answered shortly, not wanting to encourage her aunt on this subject.

"Bad memories. Can't blame Jamie for walking away from them."

From me, too?

Beth kept her mouth clamped shut. Whatever the rights and wrongs of the situation, Jamie Neilson would play no further part in her life. There was no point in rehashing memories of him. She concentrated her attention on where they were going.

The road dipped down to the creek. The wooden plank bridge rattled as they drove over it. As it had always done. They headed for the bend that curled around the knoll where the stand of spotted blue gums looked exactly the same as she remembered, their girth and height enormous compared to any she'd seen elsewhere.

Some things did last, she thought with a dark ferocity that forced her to realise how deeply she had been affected by her night with Jim Neilson. He'd recognised it rightly as a mental fight. She'd wanted so much for Jamie to emerge.

It was easy to say—put it behind her. It was harder to do.

They rounded the knoll and there was the first boundary fence of their old farm. No cattle in the fields. Nevertheless, in her mind's eye, Beth could see her brother Chris, rounding up the cows, her father taking bales of hay out to them on the tractor. She had good, warm memories of her years here. Memories Jim Neilson could have acknowledged if there'd been anything left of Jamie in him.

Forget it, she savagely berated herself. That was dead. Whereas, if she succeeded in buying back the property, she hoped it would put some vital interest into her father's life. The family was dispersed now, nothing to hold them in Melbourne. If her father could come here...well, it might make all the difference to him.

The auction sign was prominently displayed beside the gateway to the property. As they drove in, the thick cluster of turpentines, tallowwoods and wattle trees around the bend in the creek obscured any view of the farmhouse, though they could see a row of cars parked up ahead, indicating considerable interest in the auction.

Beth checked her watch. "We've got almost two hours before the bidding starts. Will we look around first or settle on a picnic spot?"

"Whatever you like, dear," came the obliging reply.

They both gasped in shock when they saw the house. It was on its way to dereliction, as though nobody had lived in it or cared for it for many years. Aunty Em brought her car to an abrupt halt. They sat, too stunned to move, gazing in horror at the ruins of what had once been a happy homestead.

The iron roof was rusting, some of the guttering falling down, several windowpanes broken, paint peeling off, gaps in the floor planks around the verandas. The white picket fence was gone. The garden was a shambles. It looked uninhabitable.

"Well, it should go cheaply," Aunty Em said ruefully.

The death of hopeful dreams stared Beth in the face. "I can't bring Dad here."

"Might put some fighting spirit back into him. He could fix this place up. Tom was always a good handyman."

It was a thought. But was it possible? "Let's see how bad it is."

They alighted from the car and headed for the house.

"The jacaranda trees are still alive. About to come into bloom, too," Aunty Em commented.

They'd always looked so beautiful, a haze of blue around the branches and the fallen blooms carpeting the ground in blue. Beth took heart that at least they remained undamaged.

"If the bushes were pruned back properly, they'd come again," Aunty Em continued, casting her keen gardener's eye over the overgrown jungle. "Needs a lot of work, but I reckon we could get the garden as shipshape as your mother had it."

The mention of her mother brought a wave of sadness to Beth. Never again would her mother stand on the veranda of this house calling them in for supper. She had died three years after they'd moved to Melbourne, leaving them all bereft of her loving presence. Beth had taken over mothering the younger ones, especially Kevin, her darling little baby brother who'd barely survived the traumatic birth that had caused their mother's death. He'd been like her very own child. It still hurt to think about him.

The city killed Kevin, her father invariably muttered on his most despondent days. Not really true, Beth thought. Accidents could happen anywhere. But that didn't help her father's depression. He'd always hated the city.

Would he hate this, too? she wondered. Or would his pride in the past spur him into trying to restore it as best he could?

They mounted the front steps of the veranda that ran around all sides of the house. "Wide, solid verandas aren't built like this anymore," Aunty Em declared, seizing on every positive factor to bolster confidence. "A few hundred nails would tighten things up and help its stability. Be careful where you step, Beth."

It was wicked, letting the house fall to rack and ruin like this, Beth thought, angry that the bank had taken it from them. Her father might have been deep in debt, but selling the property off to someone who didn't care about it seemed immoral.

Money. That was all the banks considered. Probably all Jim Neilson considered, too. Making more and more of it. Holding the mountain top. Showing off his collected wealth as the prizes of the path he'd taken. But it didn't stop the soul scream inside. Did he know what he screamed for?

Aunty Em tapped the doorframe. "It might be a good idea to check with the auctioneer if there's a report on white ants."

"Yes," Beth agreed.

She felt like screaming as they walked through the house. It looked as though it had been vandalised. Apart from broken windowpanes, ceiling lights had been torn out, holes bashed in some of the inside walls, and what was left of the bathroom and kitchen fittings was in a dreadful state. Nevertheless, they did find out from the auctioneer that the house was still structurally solid. No white ants.

They set out their picnic by the creek. Over lunch, Beth did her best to calculate the cost of renovations. It had to be subtracted from the amount she could afford to bid on the property. When it came to money, she did not have a bottomless pocket. The income from the children's books she wrote was steady, but far from astronomical. The finance she had arranged for this purchase was close to her limit. If it wasn't enough...

The distinctive thrum of a powerful engine coming into the property distracted her. Her heart caught as she saw a black Porsche zip up to the parking area near the house. It couldn't be. He wouldn't come here. Yet tension seized her in a painful grip as she waited to see who emerged from the stylish sports car.

It was slotted in beside the other parked cars. The driver's door opened. Jim Neilson alighted, unmistakable with his closely cropped black hair and tall, solidly packed physique. He turned to look at the house, his profile too breathtakingly recognisable for Beth to entertain the slightest doubt. She stared at him, struggling to reduce the wild turmoil his unexpected arrival was stirring in her.

"Who is it?" Aunty Em asked, her curiosity obviously piqued by the attention Beth had fastened on him. She didn't know about the black Porsche and had only seen full-face press photographs. Nevertheless, she was bound to identify him sooner or later.

Heat flooded up Beth's neck and burnt her cheeks at the thought of having last night's intimacy with him revealed to her aunt. Surely he wouldn't want that any more than she would. Feeling hopelessly torn by what his presence might mean, she reluctantly faced her aunt.

"It's Jim Neilson."

"Jamie?" Amazement, swiftly followed by even keener curiosity. "He's heading for the house. Well, I'll be." A wondering shake of her head. "Why would he be interested in this property?" Her gaze switched to Beth, full of sharp-eyed speculation.

"I have no idea," Beth said, reaching for a piece of orange cake.

Her appetite was completely gone, but stuffing her mouth seemed to be the most immediate way of evading questions. Impossible to guess what was going on in Jim Neilson's mind. She didn't want to think about it. She made a show of concentrating on her notebook and the numbers she'd written down, leaving her aunt to wonder as much as she liked.

The impasse did not last long.

"Well, he didn't spend much time in the house."

Beth ignored the remark.

"He's looking at us, Beth." Excitement in her voice. Pleasure. Anticipation. "He's coming over."

Apprehension crawled down her spine and knotted her stomach. Beth had to look. Jim Neilson was making a beeline for them, leaving no doubt about his intention. His gaze had locked onto hers the moment she'd lifted it to him. She felt her heart being inexorably squeezed.

"He must have recognised you," Aunty Em cried.

"No." Beth wrenched her gaze away, fastening it defiantly on her aunt. "I told him who I was. I told him I'd be here for the auction."

Bewilderment. "Why didn't you say?"

"His reaction was not exactly positive." A vast understatement.

"So... he's had second thoughts."

"I guess we're about to find out."

At the hard tone in her voice, her aunt frowned, but Beth didn't care. Jim Neilson was not going to get to her again. She could match him in the armour-plated department. All the way.

"Beth." It was a command for her attention, quietly spoken in his deep, sexy voice.

She took her time responding, examining him from the feet up. Black Reeboks. Black jeans—the same pair he'd worn last night? No bulge in his crotch now. A white linen shirt, a collarless design, undoubtedly the product of an expensive label. Tight-lipped mouth—he wasn't liking this. Eyes smoking with heat.

"Yes?" she replied, arching her eyebrows in mocking inquiry.

"I'd like a private word with you."

"Oh? Perhaps you didn't recognise my aunt. Who used to welcome you into her home and feed you up with her freshly baked cakes and cookies."

The drawled taunt speared burning colour across his cheekbones. He turned stiffly to acknowledge the woman Beth had just identified to him. "Aunty Em. Forgive me. It's been a long time." Distant courtesy, forced out.

"Yes, it has." The agreement came slowly. Aunty Em busily appraised the grown-up version of Jamie in the flesh. "Would you like to sit down with us and have a piece of orange cake?"

"No. Thank you."

He hated this, Beth thought. Hated being faced with the past. So why had he come?

He turned to her. "You've looked through the house?" Privacy, he apparently judged, was no longer necessary.

"Yes."

"Do you still intend to bid?"

"Yes."

"Why?"

It was none of his business, but she didn't like him thinking she was crazy. "My father needs it," she answered curtly.

"The house needs a bulldozer put through it."

"Thank you for your opinion."

Her sarcasm sparked a blaze of angry resentment in his eyes. "He'll never be able to turn this into a profitable farm again."

"I know that."

"Then what's the point, Beth?"

She wasn't going to explain her father's state of mind to him. He would probably consider it weak. Her eyes flared defiance of his attitude. "Some people put things behind them. Others don't. Let's leave it at that, shall we?"

They glared at each other, the silence stretching, tension loaded with fury and frustration.

"Where's your dog, Jamie?" Aunty Em asked.

His head jerked to her, a vexed rejection of the old name written on his face.

"He's Jim now, Aunty Em," Beth corrected her dryly.

"Names are neither here nor there," she said airily. "I want to know where his dog is."

"I don't have a dog." A curt statement, putting an end to the subject.

Aunty Em gave him her knowing, motherly look. "You always had a dog at your heels, Jamie Neilson. Never went anywhere without one."

"Times change," he said coldly.

"They do." Em gave slow agreement, her keen brown eyes probing and questioning before she added, "I usually find that people don't."

She was wrong, Beth thought. Jim Neilson was living proof of radical change.

He shrugged. "I have no room in my life for a dog."

"There are some things you shouldn't throw out with the bathwater," Aunty Em advised quietly. "A companion you can trust. One who loves with unquestioning devotion."

His jaw tightened. He inclined his head in mocking homage to her opinion, then pointedly returned his attention to Beth.

"You could have told me who you were," he said, accusation implicit in his tone. "At any time you could have told me."

And stopped him. That was what was burning up his guts, the fact she'd given him enough rope to hang himself with instead of letting him know her place in his life.

"Are you blaming me for the man you are?" she asked.

"What have *you* become, Beth?" he challenged, his eyes searing hers with the knowledge of how she'd acted when trying to draw him out.

She was no longer the innocent child he'd known. That was true enough. She shrugged and drawled, "Just someone who lost the plot. I guess it comes from dreaming too much."

He nodded towards the house. "Another dream?"

"Yes."

"So be it, then."

He delivered those words as though washing his hands of her. He gave her no time for a comeback, either. With a curt nod at Aunty Em, he turned and strode towards the house.

The air around them slowly cleared of electricity, leaving Beth oddly deflated. She forced a bright air of having washed her hands of him.

"We'd better pack up our picnic, Aunty Em. The auction will start soon."

"Yes," she agreed absent-mindedly, still looking after Jim Neilson. "I wonder if he'll bid."

Beth laughed derisively. "What for? To put a bulldozer through the place and raze it to the ground? Wipe out a few more memories?"

Her aunt gave her a long, thoughtful look. "Very interesting," she murmured, then busied herself storing everything in the picnic basket.

Beth didn't ask what was so interesting. She fiercely wished the auction was over, that this day was over. She didn't want to see Jim Neilson again as long as she lived. It was pride that had brought him here. He wanted to shift blame for his behaviour onto her. She'd pricked his precious self-image, and he was smarting.

Nothing but pride.

CHAPTER SEVEN

CHAIRS had been placed on the western veranda. Beth and her aunt settled in the fourth row, wanting to watch the action as well as be part of it once the bidding began. Jim Neilson was nowhere to be seen. Nevertheless, Beth was acutely aware he was still somewhere in the vicinity—the black Porsche hadn't gone—and was probably waiting to see the result of the auction.

It filled her with angry resentment. Why couldn't he leave her alone? There was no point to his hanging around. He'd said what he'd come to say, hadn't he? She certainly didn't need—or want—the distraction of his presence.

She felt wretchedly on edge as the introductory formalities were dealt with. When the auctioneer invited someone to start the bidding, her mouth was too dry to utter anything intelligible. On hearing two other people bid, she realised there was no desperate hurry to become involved.

She listened while struggling to attain the casual and relaxed attitude displayed by the other bidders, all of them men. Their faces gave nothing away. She had no idea if they were serious contenders or people out for a bargain if it went that way.

Bidders dropped out as the price rose. With a shake of their heads or a shrug of the shoulders they turned aside to murmur to their companions. Two stood firm and carried on, one of them with the darkly tanned, weathered look of a farmer, the other a short, fat, red-faced man with carbuncles on the back of his neck.

The farmer suddenly gave up. With a shock, Beth realised she had to speak now. Her bid came out in an eager rush, and she flushed, knowing she had revealed her inexperience. Her competitor raised the figure in a matter-of-fact tone. Beth calmed herself as best she could and bid again in a crisper, more businesslike voice.

Each time her competitor spoke, she waited several moments, then raised his bid, desperately hoping he would think better of making the purchase. She didn't know what his limit was, but hers was fast approaching. Beth couldn't bring herself to look at him. She willed him to give up. He didn't. His next response was the same as all the others, deadpan, remorseless, killing her hopes and killing them quickly.

There was no room left to manoeuvre. She would have one more bid, and then, on the increments that had been used so far, her opponent would bid the figure that was her limit. If only she had entered the bidding one round earlier, the situation would have been reversed. It was unthinkable, unbearable that this man could buy the property on what was *her* limit.

She didn't want him to have it. This place belonged to her family. Her father's soul was in this land, this house. If the carbuncle man bought it, he would think like Jim Neilson and bring in a bulldozer. She was sure he would. He wouldn't place any value on a broken old house that meant nothing to him.

She put in what would be her last bid. As though coming from a well-drilled martinet, the response, as with every other time, was immediate and resolute. Her heart sank. She had calculated that amount to the very last cent. She couldn't go higher, and yet the forces compelling her to go on were so strong they were irresistible. If she made one more bid, it could be the clincher.

Aunty Em leaned over and whispered, "Go again. I've got a little nest egg."

The auctioneer was looking at her.

Aunty Em squeezed her hand reassuringly.

Beth gave it one last shot, willing it to be the winning bid.

It wasn't.

The carbuncle man topped it.

Her aunt gave a sad shake of her head. Beth swallowed, her mind racing wildly to find ways and means, yet sanity insisted it would be totally foolhardy to go on. Limits were limits. Getting into hopeless debt had lost this farm in the first place. What good would it do to place herself and her father in that position again?

She slumped in her chair, defeated and drowning in disappointment. However unfair it seemed to her that someone else was buying the property, she had to accept it. The chance was gone, and there was nothing she could do about it.

The auctioneer started his wind-up patter. As expected, there were no more bids. The gavel fell for the first time. It fell a second time. It was on its downward swing for the third and final time when...

"Five thousand more."

Jim Neilson's voice!

Shocked, Beth spun around in her chair. She wasn't the only one startled, either. There was a general shifting, every head turning to see who had entered the bidding at this late stage.

He was leaning against a veranda post at the back of the gathering, looking relaxed and easy, uncaring of the interest he'd drawn. If anything, he exuded boredom with the proceedings. Only the derisive glint in his eyes as he briefly met Beth's stunned look revealed a sense of purpose. For the rest, he was poker-faced.

Beth swung to watch the carbuncle man, who must have thought the property was in his pocket. Unaccountably, her heart was pounding. She didn't know what she wanted to happen, but there was a dreadful fascination in seeing who would come out the winner.

The man who'd bested her was disturbed by this new development, eyeing Jim Neilson as though he was a snake in the grass. Impossible to know if he connected his new competitor to the black Porsche, but even in the lazy stance by the veranda post, there was an air of command, the air of a person who got what he wanted.

Reluctant to give up, Beth's opponent increased the bid by two thousand, testing the waters.

"Another five," came the casual response, as though the amount meant absolutely nothing to Jim Neilson. It seeded the impression he could just as easily have said ten or twenty, and would, if that's what it took to secure the deal.

The carbuncle man grimaced and shook his head at the auctioneer, indicating withdrawal. If he wasn't financially beaten, he was certainly psychologically beaten, Beth thought, getting a glimpse of how formidable Jim Neilson must be in business dealings. A sleek shark, moving in and hitting hard when least expected.

She shivered at the image. The realisation struck her. It was precisely what he had done last night, moving in unexpectedly, then raising the level of the encounter with mind-boggling increments—the swift sweep out of the gallery, the kiss by the car, his boldness in the elevator. Winning was definitely Jim Neilson's game. But what did he anticipate winning by buying this property?

Beth sat burning with frustration as the auctioneer wound up the sale. She didn't want to speak to Jim Neilson again, but she had to know what he intended to do with the farm. He couldn't actually want it.

The people around her started moving, ready to leave now the action was over. Jim Neilson was conferring with the auctioneer, no doubt discussing the formal paperwork to seal the deal. She should have been doing that, Beth thought, tasting the bitterness of defeat again. It drove her to her feet, unable to bear watching any more.

She managed a twisted smile for her aunt, who looked at her with a slightly befuddled air. "Thanks for trying to help, Aunty Em. Let's get moving now."

"Don't you think we should wait?" She gestured towards the auctioneer's table.

"Not here," Beth said decisively, aware that her aunt was entertaining questions about Jim Neilson's intentions, too.

"As you like, dear." The concession was quick, making Beth wonder if her tension was obvious to all eyes.

Jim Neilson didn't so much as glance in their direction as they made their way past the rows of chairs to the end of the veranda. Beth was glad to turn the corner and put him out of sight. It disturbed her that she felt so strongly linked to him.

The carbuncle man was holding forth to an associate by the front steps. "The man's a fool. It's not worth that much. He hasn't got a hope in hell of turning it over for a profit."

Money, Beth thought in disgust. A property investor out to make a quick buck. Her feeling about him had been right. He saw this land as a commodity, nothing else.

The question to be answered was how Jim Neilson saw it. From his earlier stated opinions, there seemed no reason for him to pay more than the property was worth in land value. There had to be some motive behind his acquiring a farm he couldn't possibly want.

Beth chewed over this until they were clear of the neglected garden. "What do you think, Aunty Em?" she asked, tormented into seeking another perception of Jim Neilson's decisive action.

"I think we should have a cup of coffee. I packed a second thermos. And there's plenty of cake left."

"I meant about the outcome of the auction."

"Well, dear, I don't know what went on between you and Jamie last night...." She paused to give Beth an arch look.

Beth chose not to enlighten her.

"But from what I heard and observed in your exchange with him earlier this afternoon—" a self-conscious flush swept up Beth's neck "—I think he bought the farm for you."

The flush turned into a painful burn. "I couldn't accept it from him." The words shot out of her mouth with vehement emphasis.

Aunty Em made no comment, leaving Beth to stew over her response as they walked to the car.

It was voiced now, the thought that had been knocking at her mind from the moment Jim Neilson had made his first bid. Beth hadn't wanted to admit it. If it was true, he was continuing the mental fight, turning the tables on her, giving her the dream he was capable of delivering.

And maybe—just maybe—if she'd stopped him last night with the truth of who she was ... No, she couldn't concede he would have been different. He might have made a superficial effort to be nice to her, but it wouldn't have changed the man inside.

He didn't like being put in the wrong. Pride, that was it. So he hadn't lived up to his word in one area. With what he had achieved, he could compensate by handing her something else, balance the ledger with his damned chequebook. But there was no heart in money. No soul. It was a commodity he had in plenty. No pain to use it.

Beth was seething with these thoughts as her aunt busied herself with the picnic basket. When she was handed a cup of coffee, she took it absent-mindedly, murmuring an automatic thanks. She shook her head at the offering of cake. Impossible to eat with her stomach in knots.

Cars were starting to leave.

Beth sneaked a look at the house. A man was stacking the portable chairs on the veranda, loading them into a pick-up truck. Behind him a group of people remained around the auctioneer's table.

"Perhaps you could work out a deal with Jamie."

"Deal?" Beth repeated, looking blankly at her aunt.

"Terms by which you can manage to pay back the money."

"I don't want any favours from him, Aunty Em," Beth said harshly.

She earned a long, soul-searching look from her aunt. "Do you want the farm, Beth?" she asked quietly.

"You know I do." She gestured helplessness with her dilemma.

"I've always thought pride costs more than it's worth. People lose things they really want through pride. Then they rue it for the rest of their lives."

Beth frowned, inwardly recoiling from acknowledging her aunt's wisdom, yet unable to dismiss the truth in it. Reluctantly she said, "It would mean owing him."

A wry shrug. "Perhaps Jamie feels he owes you."

Having voiced this thought, her aunt turned aside to gaze at the creek as she munched on a piece of cake, leaving Beth to ponder the situation further.

Pride. His, hers ...

Shouldn't her father's need override both?

She drank her coffee as she tried to get her priorities straightened out. Her mind was still darting through a mass of warring emotions when she flicked another glance at the house and caught sight of Jim Neilson at the top of the front steps, looking directly at her.

The sense of being stripped naked again by him stirred internal mayhem. It was as though she felt the powerful force of his mind, the absolute self-assurance of being in command, ready to dictate his terms. Her heart kicked into a faster beat to accommodate the need for more oxygen to the brain. Her mind fiercely challenged his to one hell of a fight.

He moved down the steps in a leisurely stroll, knowing there was no hurry. She was waiting for him. Another battleground, and he had the territory she wanted. The controlling hand. It emanated from him so strongly, Beth knew she was not mistaken.

So much for any feeling that he owed her something, she thought in savage derision. Aunty Em's thinking was influenced by her memories of Jamie. She didn't know this man, hadn't experienced him as Beth had. There was no quarter given by Jim Neilson.

"Have you finished your coffee, dear?" Aunty Em inquired.

"Yes."

Beth wrenched her gaze off her deadly antagonist to hand over her empty cup. She watched her aunt pack and close the picnic basket. They could go right now, leave Jim Neilson to an empty victory. Just get in the car and go. If the carbuncle man had won the auction, they'd be doing precisely that, not waiting for Jim Neilson's next move.

Yet to go was a defeat, too. She had to face this out. Seize some initiative herself. "I'm going to talk to him, Aunty Em," she said decisively, and pushed her feet into action.

He was heading for his Porsche. He had a sheaf of papers in his hand, a contract for the sale, no doubt. Beth's heart pumped overtime as the distance closed between them. He halted first, letting her come to him, his eyes running down her outfit to her sensible walking shoes and up again, a sardonic little smile playing on his mouth, making him look infinitely dangerous.

Payback time, Beth thought, gritting her teeth, determined not to reveal the physical effect he had on her. She stopped a good metre from him, acutely conscious of the need to keep space between them. She didn't trust Jim Neilson not to take some sneaky advantage.

"Are you pleased with your new acquisition?" she asked.

"I hope it will serve its purpose," he answered noncommittally.

"It was a high price to pay."

He shrugged. "Irrelevant to me."

"It must be nice not to have to count the cost of what you want."

"Oh, I count it, Beth. I always count everything. That's how I got to be where I am."

He was fencing, and she was getting nowhere. "Aunty Em has the idea that you took over the bidding for me," she stated bluntly.

"Well, she could be right." He was enjoying teasing her. "What do you think?"

It incensed her into snapping, "Why don't you tell me and get it over with?"

The teasing sparkle hardened to a ruthless glitter. "Perhaps I don't want to get it over with. Is it such a hardship to talk to me, Beth? We were once friends, remember? And might have been again if you'd approached me openly. Honestly."

"We've moved beyond friendship. You decided that many years ago, Jim Neilson. You can't play that game with me."

He saw the cutting edge in her eyes and shifted ground. "You want this farm."

"You know I do."

"For your father."

"Yes."

"Then travel to Sydney with me and we'll talk about it."

It sounded so innocuous, yet Beth's skin prickled with the sense of danger. In his car. In his power. On the other hand, what else could he do but talk if he was driving? And if she could strike some acceptable bargain with him, wasn't it worth a bit of heartburn on her part to give her father back the life he yearned for?

Jim Neilson watched her consider his offer, his eyes mocking her caution. It goaded Beth into asking, "What do you think you're buying with me?"

"Time," he answered blandly.

She knew she wouldn't get any more out of him at this juncture. As far as she could see, she had nothing of any importance to lose by going with him, and everything to gain.

"All right. Please excuse me while I fix it with Aunty Em."

Beth felt his gaze burning into her back with every step she took away from him. Was he stripping her again, remembering how she had looked, standing at his window last night? What did he want from her now?

There was only one certainty in Beth's mind.

Jim Neilson wanted something from her, and he intended to use the time he'd won to get it.

CHAPTER EIGHT

JIM wanted to kill her.

He wanted to smash her cool control into irretrievable pieces.

He wanted to hurl her to the ground and use her as she'd used him to get this worthless piece of land.

He hated her for being the kind of woman she was, instead of... But that Beth didn't exist, he savagely reminded himself, and he shouldn't be letting this bitch of a woman needle him. Why the hell hadn't he just slapped the papers in her hand, then got in his car and driven away?

Dragging it on was stupid!

He wrenched his gaze away from her, locked the papers in the car and set off for the creek, needing to walk off the violent feelings she stirred. He was still burning from the way she'd looked at him when he'd arrived, like a stud who'd serviced her and could now be discarded.

Well, she could damned well wait for what she wanted!

He was nobody's sucker.

Though she'd done one favour for him.

She'd killed off the dream of Beth once and for all.

It wouldn't haunt him any more.

CHAPTER NINE

TIME!

Beth seethed over the loophole she had not foreseen in Jim Neilson's seemingly harmless request for her to accompany him to Sydney. He intended taking more time than that. He was doing it already, deliberately making her wait, knowing she had no means to change her mind about the agreement now that Aunty Em had gone.

It infuriated her even more that he was lounging on the creek bank, underneath the old red gum that designated the best swimming hole. She didn't believe for one moment he was entertaining memories of the fun times they'd had there as children. It was a tactic to draw her to him and have as much *time* as he wanted with her.

Beth stayed by the Porsche. He'd locked the doors, so she couldn't sit in it. The sale papers from the auction lay on the driver's seat, a tantalising reminder of why she was here. Jim Neilson certainly knew how to turn the screw. But she would not play his game. He could whistle for her to join him on the creek bank as much as he liked. She would not go.

The pick-up truck carrying the auction furniture zoomed off down the road. She watched the rest of the cars leave one by one, each departure increasing her tension. The idea of being isolated with Jim Neilson had no appeal.

Not that she was afraid of him. It simply made her feel more vulnerable than she liked to be. She couldn't deny there was a strong attraction, and it disturbed her that he had the power to push physical buttons she'd prefer to ignore.

When the last car disappeared around the bend to the gateway, Beth had to fight a sense of oppression. The Porsche sat alone. She stood alone. And Jim Neilson was stretched out on the grass, hands behind his head, totally at ease with himself.

Determinedly gathering some purpose of her own, Beth set off for the house. It had taken on its abandoned air again. She skirted it, looking at it from every angle, visualising it as it had once been, as it could be again with enough work and care and love. Yet was it too big a project for her father? Would it depress him further, or as Aunty Em said, bring out his fighting spirit? She could be on a fool's errand with Jim Neilson, achieving nothing whichever way it went.

At least the concrete water tanks were intact. She washed her hands under the outside tap and splashed water on her face to make her feel fresher. It had been a long, wearisome day. And was getting longer.

Having trekked around the house, she sat on the front steps and tried to relax. Two could play at the waiting game. She was not going to stand by the Porsche, looking as though she was fretting over Jim Neilson's inactivity. Eventually he would have to move, and she would meet him at the car.

Time dragged on. Beth began to wonder if he'd dozed off in the lingering warmth of the afternoon and the peaceful silence of the country. They hadn't slept much last night. She winced at the memory of how they had filled those hours, neither of them calling a halt. Several times they had drifted into a languorous sleep...until one or the other of them moved, and the compulsion to reach out came again and again.

Beth heaved a sigh to relieve the tightness in her chest. Jim Neilson's hands were no longer under his head. His arms were sprawled at his sides. He didn't look at all dangerous, flat on his back like that. Perhaps she had done him an injustice, thinking he was playing some devious tactic. He might simply have needed to close his eyes for a while before facing the drive to Sydney. Fatigue could be a killer on the road.

She checked her watch. It was over an hour since everyone had gone. Her bottom was stiff from sitting on the hard, wooden step. She decided it wouldn't be weak on her part to wander down to the creek bank. In fact, it was perfectly reasonable to wake him up if he'd fallen asleep. The sun was beginning to set. He could hardly expect her to wait around for hours, especially with twilight coming soon.

He didn't so much as twitch as she approached. Fast asleep. She watched him for a while, tracing Jamie in his adult face, feeling a strange mixture of emotions. An intimate stranger, she thought, wishing there was some way to recapture the rapport they had once shared. Or had she somehow exaggerated that in her memory? Whatever...it was gone.

He'd rolled up his sleeves. On sheer impulse, Beth leaned down, snapped off a stalk of paspalum and brushed its head along the inner side of his outstretched arm, smiling at the childish action. It should tease him into stirring. She could drop the stalk before his eyes opened and he wouldn't know what had set his nerves tingling.

He moved so quickly, so unexpectedly, Beth was caught hopelessly off balance. A yank on her foot and she was toppling. Somehow he directed her fall so she landed on top of him, and before she could take any action, his arms were around her and they were rolling, her long, voluminous skirt winding around them, pinning them together as she landed on her back with Jim Neilson's face hovering above hers.

'Mmm...I remember this,' he said in a low, throaty purr, slumberous eyes simmering briefly at her before his mouth descended on hers, stifling any shocked protest she might have made.

Instinctively bracing herself against a storming invasion, Beth clamped her teeth together, denying him entry. But he didn't try to kiss her like that. His lips beguiled hers with seductive little nibbles, his tongue sliding over the inner tissues, arousing electric tingles that dizzied her outrage at his trickery. Or perhaps it was lack of oxygen draining her of the fury she should feel. His weight had knocked the breath out of her.

She tried to fight the confusing signals in her mind. He had to be stopped from taking these liberties with her. His chest was squashing her breasts, making them extremely sensitive to the muscular wall pressing down on them. Her hands were pinned between their bodies, too close to his groin to attempt wriggling them. She was far too conscious of that part of his anatomy as it was. Impossible to move her legs. Her skirt was wrapped around them like a straitjacket. With his mouth teasing hers, waiting for her to open it, she couldn't risk speaking.

"I've been wanting to taste you again all day," he murmured, momentarily relinquishing his advantage.

"Get off me!" she said angrily.

He grinned at her, his dark eyes dancing with sheer wickedness. "You're much softer than the ground, Beth. If you didn't want this, you shouldn't have woken me with a caress."

She tried to lick away the tingle on her lips, fiercely resenting the physical effect he had on her. It was a mistake. His gaze dropped to her mouth again. In an instant his tongue was riding hers, taking free passage and infiltrating her defensive system in one fell swoop. The sensory attack was so fast it fused Beth's mind with a power overload. A primitive response kicked in, her mouth returning the oral assault with passionate fury, her whole body bucking in violent need to assert herself as an equally potent force.

He rolled to put her astride him. For a moment she exulted in the release from his embrace, the sense of freedom. But as she tugged at her skirt, trying to hitch it out of its entanglement with her legs, his hands opened her shirt and swept it off her shoulders. He hooked his thumbs into her bra straps and dragged them down her arms, as well.

"Damn you! Why can't you let me be?" she yelled at him, grabbing his wrists too late as he scooped her breasts out of the loosened cups of lace.

His eyes glittered at her, ablaze with raw desire. 'And miss out on these?' he asked. "So lusciously full and soft. Incredibly sexy. They're inviting me to eat them."

She looked down, distracted by the hard puckering of her nipples. It was the cool air on them, she wildly reasoned, fighting the excitement of his words.

"You want control?" he challenged. "Stay on top. Feed them to me."

She was tempted. Some pagan streak soared through her blood, pounded through her temples. The image of riding this man as he paid slavish homage to her breasts had a savage appeal. Out in the open, under the sky, grass beneath them, a breeze whispering through the leaves overhead, the setting sun pouring red streaks through the clouds... raw nature. It was as though her senses leapt into another dimension, demanding a satisfaction that was beyond any civilised rule.

She slid her hands down his forearms, her nails lightly clawing his skin, her eyes agleam with the golden vision of making him do her will, burning with the command, *wait for me*. She leaned over him, placing her palms flat on the ground on either side of his head. She felt the swell of his chest as he dragged in a deep breath, but apart from that instinctive need he lay still, watching her, captivated by the swiftly passing expressions on her face, crystallising into a glittering lust for vengeful domination.

"Now, catch me if you can," she challenged and swung her body from side to side, offering her breasts to his mouth in such fast tandem, he could barely grab one before it was torn away and he was taunted with the other. She laughed at the sheer erotic madness of it, the thrill of the chase and the capture, the pumping excitement that drove her to wild excess.

With a deep, animal growl, he hurled her onto her back, rolling to hold her down, hands on her shoulders to keep her still as he took his time with the flesh she had offered him, pleasuring her so piercingly that she wrapped her hands around his head to encourage more and more frantic activity.

Her legs moved restlessly, knees prodding, feet trying to find purchase. He reared up from her, unfastened his jeans, dragged up her skirt, and she devoured the look on his face, the taut need, the flare of out-of-control wanting, and she moved her body sensuously, invitingly, driving him into fumbling with his protection in his haste to serve his desire.

No patience for undressing. No wish for finesse. Only the craving for a fast fix to compelling need. He pushed her panties aside and plunged himself into the seething cauldron of heat that welcomed him as fiercely as he entered it, the most primal mating of a male and female, the pounding sensation of drumming flesh and hearts in a rhythm that shattered into an ecstatic oblivion, where the external world lost all existence, and through the sudden and complete annihilation of all emotions and desires drifted a passionless peace.

How long she lay suspended in some timeless nirvana Beth didn't know. Her eyes opened. She gradually focused on the long twisted limb that grew out of the old red gum and stretched across the creek. In the old days her father had hung a rope from it so all the kids could play Tarzan. Or Jane.

It occurred to Beth that Tarzan and Jane could not have been more primitive in their sexual play than the action that had just taken place on the bank of this creek. Though Beth imagined there would have been love and affection in their coupling, not some crazy lust that took possession of them. She felt like a stranger to herself, almost as though she was having an out-of-body experience, except for Jim Neilson lending a hot, heavy, physical weight to it.

He shifted, as though awareness was gradually seeping into the groggy aftermath of absolute chaos for him, too. Very slowly he lifted himself away to lie beside her. She didn't look at him. It was too much effort. She didn't want to, anyway. He might have planned something like this, but she hadn't. She'd fallen into it. Her mind groped for understanding. What was it in him that called out such a shockingly carnal side of her?

She had excused it last night, telling herself it was a means to an end. Impossible to excuse its emergence today. What prompted such wild lust? Was it some uncontrollable chemistry, only needing the stimulus of sexual attraction to ignite it? She couldn't deny Jim Neilson's physical impact on her. But there was something mental, too. Like a snap in her brain, a door springing open to spaces that demanded filling.

But why him?

If it had been Jamie...

He was Jamie.

No, he wasn't. Not how she remembered him, anyway. Or was she remembering the wrong things, missing the real core?

He'd always had the streak in him to dare, to push everything to its limits. He'd been more exciting to be with than any other kid in the valley. He made things happen, invented them, filled her head with wild fantasies. Around him, everything was fast and intense. Yet he'd been protective, too, watching out for her, caring.

That was what was lacking now, the caring. It was all take. Still exciting, but on the wrong level, making her feel wrong about it once the excitement was over.

He suddenly hoisted himself to his feet and without a word to her walked along the bank a bit to attend to himself and adjust his clothing. Beth hurriedly did the same, needing to somehow maintain equal ground with him. Out of the corner of her eye she saw him turn and stare thoughtfully at her, as though assessing the situation between them. He was too calculating, Beth thought resentfully.

"Ready to go?" he asked when she'd finished buttoning her shirt.

"Whenever you are," she returned crisply.

He strode to where her handbag had been dropped, picked it up and held it out to her. His mouth tilted into a lopsided grin that was oddly boyish as she took the bag from him.

"You are one hell of a woman, Beth Delaney," he said with what sounded suspiciously like relish.

She stared directly into his brilliant dark eyes, not cracking so much as a smile. "Do you prefer hell to heaven?"

He laughed and turned towards the car. "I gave up believing in heaven a long time ago."

"Yes. I guess you did," she agreed, falling into step beside him.

He was hard, cynical and self-sufficient apart from needing an obliging partner to satisfy his sexual drive. On his terms. Beth felt quite certain Jim Neilson no more believed in love than he believed in heaven. He wouldn't promise it, either. He wouldn't stoop to that kind of dishonesty. There was a rough kind of integrity in the challenge he undoubtedly threw out to women. *Take me as I am or walk away*.

But he had pursued *her*.

Though what that meant Beth was yet to find out.

At least the crackling tension between them had eased, she thought, wryly putting that down to the sexual release they had shared. It was almost a companionable walk to the Porsche. Jim Neilson unlocked and opened the passenger door for her with casual courtesy. She stepped in without hesitation or apprehension. Impossible to imagine anything of any great moment happening that could top what had already happened.

She fastened her seat belt and relaxed into the comfortable leather seat as he rounded the car to the driver's side. He opened the door, bent down, picked up the papers from his seat and tossed them onto her lap.

"Yours," he said, as he settled behind the driving wheel.

"What do you mean, mine?" she asked, frowning at the legal papers pertaining to the sale of the property.

He closed his door, fastened his seat belt, switched on the engine and thrummed up the revs before he answered her. "You wanted this property. I bought it for you. It's yours, free and clear."

He gave her a sizzling look to confirm his gift, then gunned the motor and swung his Porsche away from the house he had paid for, speeding down the road to the gateway, away from the land he didn't want, heading fast out of the valley he preferred to forget.

CHAPTER TEN

Shock kept Beth silent. She was vaguely aware of valley landmarks flashing past them, but her mind was in too much turmoil to take them in as she had during the drive with Aunty Em. Jamie—Jim—made no comment on anything. He was probably waiting for some response from her. His gift of her old family property certainly rated one.

"Why?" she finally asked.

He shrugged and slanted her a sardonic smile. "I can afford it."

"I don't doubt you can, but...that doesn't answer my question."

A sharp, hard probe from dark, fathomless eyes. "Does it matter to you?"

"Yes," she answered vehemently. "I can't just accept—" she gestured agitatedly "—so much."

"Why not?"

"I wouldn't feel right about it."

He pondered that response for a while, then gave her a derisive look. "I accepted a lot from you and your family in years gone by."

Aunty Em's words flashed into Beth's mind. *Perhaps Jamie feels he owes you.*

She shook her head. It was wrong to reduce kindness and consideration and friendship to some mercenary level. To offer chequebook generosity to clear some perceived debt seemed almost offensive to the spirit of including him in their family fold.

"None of what was given to you by my family was ever given with the thought of being repaid," she asserted strongly, her distress at the idea creeping into her voice as she added, "surely you know that!"

"Of course I do," he agreed easily. "None of you could have possibly foreseen that I'd ever amount to anything."

The lightly mocking tone set her nerves on edge again. It was a more subtle fight, but he *was* fencing with her, not letting her into his mind. She sensed her words were bouncing off his habitual suit of armour, not penetrating at all. Jim Neilson was on his own somewhere, as unreachable as ever.

"Though it's been quite amazing how many people have climbed out of the woodwork since I have proved worth knowing," he drawled. "People who've had no contact with me for years. People I don't even recognise." He flashed her an ironic smile. "Usually they want something from me."

Beth flushed in mortification as she realised what he was implying, what he thought!

"Sometimes I give it. Sometimes I don't," he went on, his tone hardening. "I guess you knew that."

"No. I didn't," she protested, almost swallowing the words, shrinking from the cynicism she realised was based on experiences that would sour even a giving heart.

She'd had no idea he'd been pestered by people for handouts on the basis of having known him in less fortunate circumstances. It appalled her that he was putting her in the same class—a parasite on the fortune he'd made for himself.

"You of all people could have come to me straight, Beth. You didn't have to bait the hook."

Bait the hook? She stared at him incredulously, her flush heating into a painful burn at his interpretation of her actions. He was putting her in the same class as a whore who used sexual performance to draw what she wanted out of a client. And it was true in a way, though it hadn't been money on her mind. Never money.

He gave a dark chuckle. "I must say I'm glad you did. I wouldn't have missed last night and this afternoon for anything. You are one hell of a woman."

"So you said," she muttered bitterly, sickened by his view of her. It was so twisted, horrible. Her self-respect demanded she correct it. "Let me get this straight, Jim Neilson. You think I played you along to draw you into providing backup finance in case I couldn't buy the farm."

His eyes glittered briefly at her. "Don't keep playing me for a fool, Beth. I'll admit I've never been on the receiving end of a more masterly piece of manipulation. It was psychologically brilliant. You had me skidding down a guilt trip this morning."

She hadn't planned it. Not any of it. Her heart was pumping furiously. It was difficult to keep her mind clear, to pursue this abomination right down the line.

"But you'd reasoned it all out by the time you got to the farm," she prompted, remembering the searing look in his eyes as he'd mockingly asked, *What have you become*?

"That's what I do best. Add up all the factors forming market forces and use the emerging pattern as a springboard to jump ahead of everyone else in foreseeing where the profit's going to be."

"Don't you ever make a mistake?"

"Not often, and never a big one."

Welcome to a huge one, buster! "I see," she said, covering her inner seething with a calm, matter-of-fact tone. "So where is the profit in this deal for you?"

He didn't answer immediately.

"You're giving me the property. What do you get?" she prodded.

A smile lurked on his lips.

She hated him.

"Free of guilt?" she mocked.

He laughed. "You excite me more than any woman I've ever met. And the feeling's mutual." His eyes threw her a hot challenge. "Isn't it, Beth?"

Impossible to deny, even though she was sizzling with rage. She fixed her attention on the road, letting her silence seed doubts in him. If he ever allowed himself doubts. She wanted to pour scorn on his head, attack him tooth and claw for drawing such a sleazy picture of her, but she'd given the primitive streak in her too much rein as it was. Now was the time for rigid control, cool dignity, unshakable resolution.

They were out of the valley. The road sign directing them onto the expressway was right ahead of them. She had to play her cards right to get rid of Jim Neilson. He was a burr under her skin that had to be torn out. She'd patch over the wound somehow once she was free of him.

"It's not over," he said as though acknowledging it to himself. "Maybe it will burn itself out in time. Who knows? As I see it, we take it as far as it goes."

Buying time!

"That's the profit, is it?" She managed an ironic smile. "You bought the farm to keep me on as your sexual partner."

"Let's say the farm is more accessible to Sydney than Melbourne is. For both of us."

"A love nest?" she mocked.

"Hardly. With your father there." He shot her a smouldering look. "Would it be a hardship for you to drive to Sydney? I'm sure you could invent the occasional errand."

Of course, she thought derisively. Jim Neilson didn't want to come to the valley. Bad karma for him. He thought he was in the box seat, having handed over her father's dream on a plate, and he was now spelling out his terms. Jim Neilson wasn't about to come down from his mountain. He wanted her on top of it. Until she wasn't *exciting* any more.

They zoomed onto the expressway, and with a bit of deft handling, the Porsche was swiftly steered into the fast lane. Naturally. Nothing slow for this man.

"I suppose I should feel flattered you paid so much for me," she said, her voice projecting light amusement. "It's nice to know my value."

It earned a glowering look. "I'm not buying you. I simply wanted you satisfied."

"Oh, I am." Knowing what was in his mind cleared up all the mystery for her. She let a smile linger on her lips as she looked at his thighs, deliberately holding her gaze there as she added, "Though I think you underrate yourself. You're quite a pistol, Jim."

She sensed him weighing the comment, sifting it from every angle, doing his brand of mathematics on it. Nevertheless, there probably wasn't a man alive who didn't respond positively to having his virility tagged with dynamic potency. Beth looked away, wishing she could castrate him. Which just went to prove he was still striking some savage strain in her.

"Are you staying with your aunt in Sydney?"

There was calculation behind that question. No doubt he wanted to show her his pistol was a six-shooter. *Is he riding for a fall*! Beth thought viciously. And she was just the person to make the fall as hard as it could be!

"No. I'm by myself. Staying at the Ramada Hotel in Ryde," she answered casually.

"Are you free to have dinner with me?"

The wolf's appetite was whetted. "In your apartment again?" she asked pointedly.

A wicked grin, twinkling with arrogant confidence. "We could pick up some food along the way. What do you like? Italian? Chinese? Indian?"

"I take it you don't want to hang around in a restaurant," she said dryly, reading him with ease. Why waste time when he could be feeding every appetite?

A flick of eyes already simmering with anticipation. "Not as intimate. But if you'd prefer it..."

He was prepared to wait an hour or two. "Sometimes it pays not to rush," she said, loading the words with suggestive meaning.

He liked it. She could feel his delight, excitement building, the imaginative leap to sexual flirtation over and under a table in a public restaurant. It lent an extra edge to what would follow. Little did he know he was about to be paid out for rushing into judgment on her!

"Where would you like to go?" he asked.

Beth cynically supposed money could find a table for two in most restaurants, even though it was a Saturday night and the more fashionable and popular places would be fully booked. "Let me think about it," she said, leaving the promise hanging.

The Porsche was eating up the road. At the rate they were travelling, the outskirts of Sydney were not far away. Another twenty minutes or so. She needed to soak up time to play out her hand for maximum impact.

He gave her five minutes before prompting, "Tell me what you fancy. If you don't know many places in Sydney..."

"I don't. Better for you to decide." She offered him a teasing smile. "Surprise me. You're very good at that."

"You have quite a talent for it yourself," he said with an appreciative sparkle.

Wait for it, lover, she silently commanded him. "I want to go to my hotel first. I'd like to change out of these clothes."

"First stop, the Ramada," he readily agreed.

"It's along Epping Road."

"I know it."

"Good. Then if you don't mind, I'll close my eyes for a while. I'll be much fresher after a catnap."

"Go ahead." He gave her a teasing smile. "I'll think of a way to wake you up."

The claws would be out so fast he wouldn't see them coming.

Beth closed her eyes on that venomous thought. She didn't go to sleep. Her mind was like a bed of nails, thinking what a fool she'd been, chasing after dreams that should have been laid to rest years ago. She could certainly forget them now. Though maybe Jim Neilson would put the farm on the market once he realised it wouldn't buy what he wanted.

No reason for him to keep it. And the carbuncle man was of the opinion it would not fetch such a high price again. If she contacted the real estate company that had run the auction, let them know she was still an interested party should the new owner want to sell, a bargain might be struck at a price she could afford.

Though it would probably be wise to arrange it through some agent, not use her name. Jim Neilson was not going to like swallowing the mistake he had made. He wouldn't want her to profit by it. Wiser in the long run for her to forget the whole thing, just wipe it off the possibility register. Yet there was still her father to consider.

Sick at heart, she wished her aunt had never told her about the auction, never shown her the item in the society pages mentioning Jim Neilson as one of the invited guests to the exhibition opening at the Woollhara gallery. This whole trip had been a disaster from start to finish.

Well, not quite, she corrected herself. The visit to her publisher's Sydney office had been productive. Her books were selling so well, a larger print run was being considered. Not bad for children's books.

Jim Neilson hadn't even asked her what she did for a living. So much for any interest in her as a person! He probably thought she sponged off lovers. It was laughable, considering how few men there had been in her life. Only Gerald, in any serious sense. And why she had hung onto him for so long, she didn't know. Easier to drift than to break away?

She would have no problem breaking away from Jim Neilson!

Beth felt her jaw clenching and forced herself to relax again. They had to be in Sydney suburbia by now. The Porsche had stopped several times, signalling the occurrence of red traffic lights. It was time to get her mind into gear for the final showdown.

Jim Neilson was about to be proved right in one sense. She'd had no thought of playing him along last night or this morning, but she had certainly done it since leaving the valley. She hoped it would leave as bitter a taste in his mouth as he had left in hers. She was not a vengeful person by nature, but somehow he stirred a depth of passion that made hitting him where it hurt seem right. Necessary. Aunty Em would probably call it pride.

Beth didn't care. Jim Neilson deserved to feel like a fool. It might give him pause to reconsider his record of not making big mistakes. It would do him good to realise he wasn't so damned infallible in his calculations and judgments. For once in his life, he could count the loss, not the profit.

She stirred as though waking. "Where are we?" she asked, peering around for recognisable landmarks.

"Almost there. Coming up to the turn onto Epping Road," he answered, shooting her a quirky smile. "You woke too soon."

Not soon enough, where he was concerned. Dreams always put too rosy a complexion on things, and hope was a treacherous feeling. Reality was something else.

Beth gathered together the papers on her lap, ready for decisive action. She reached for her handbag, resting near her feet, and set it on the side of her seat closest to the door. Two more sets of traffic lights and they were turning off Epping Road, heading straight for the entrance into the hotel grounds.

Instead of continuing around the driveway to the doors leading into the foyer, the Porsche headed straight into the parking area for guests. Fortunately, there was an empty slot in a direct line with the driveway, and Jim Neilson did not look any further. Beth realised she should have anticipated the intention to accompany her to her room. Cooling his heels was not his style.

At least she didn't have far to walk. She released her seat belt, ready to move as he switched off the engine. Having slid her arm through the strap on her handbag, she opened the door.

A hand descended on her thigh, arresting movement. "I'll come with you," he said.

She stared at the hand, resenting its power to touch her and create more physical havoc than any other hand. "No, you won't," she stated with incisive emphasis.

"The waiting game can be played too far, Beth," he warned.

"I'm not playing." She lifted her gaze to his, golden daggers of scorn stabbing into the windows of his soul. "You extracted the wrong data to key into your computer, Jim Neilson. You brought up the wrong chain of logic. You made the wrong call."

He frowned. "You're not making sense."

"I didn't come to ask you for anything. It was you who made the running."

"Oh, come on."

She tossed the sale papers onto his lap. "No deal. Not now. Not ever."

While he was still caught by surprise, she pushed her door open, swung her legs around and was out of the car in one fluid motion.

"Wait!" he called, making a grab for her skirt.

She swished it out of reach and glared at him, hurling her bitterness in his face. "In the game of life, Jim Neilson, you lost the lot. Keep your precious profits. They're all empty of any heart. Like you." Then she stepped back and slammed the door.

Chin up, shoulders straight, back rigid, she marched towards the entrance to the hotel. She heard his door open and close but didn't turn her head. He strode after her and caught her by the upper arm, forcing her to a halt. Still she didn't turn, didn't look at him.

"Release me at once," she commanded, her voice seething with passionate intent. "If you follow me any further I will have you charged with harassment."

"It's stupid to cut off your nose to spite your face," he growled. "You want me as much as I want you."

"Let me go or I'll call the doorman for help. Believe me. I'll do it."

His grip slackened. "Look at me, Beth!" he demanded, his voice harsh with urgency as his hand dropped away.

"If I never see you again, it will be too soon."

Without the slightest glance his way, disdaining any further acknowledgment of him, she walked on...out of his life.

CHAPTER ELEVEN

IT WAS more an ordeal than a pleasure for Beth to sit through the elaborate Sunday lunch put on for her by Aunty Em's son, Martin, and his wife, Lorraine. Naturally they wanted to know the outcome of the auction. It seemed incomprehensible to them that she'd been unable to strike a reasonable arrangement with Jim Neilson over the property.

After all, why would he want it? And surely, even if he'd left the persona of Jamie in his past, didn't he appreciate how much the old place meant to the Delaney family?

Aunty Em, thank heaven, kept her own counsel, not joining in the round-table discussion except to say her version of *que sera*— what was not to be, was not to be. Beth was grateful for her restraint.

Eventually Beth managed to turn the conversation to happier topics. She always sent copies of her books to Martin's and Lorraine's children, and they were easily encouraged to recount which were their favourites, and why, and make their suggestions for future stories. There were times, Beth decided, when fantasies were much better than realities.

It was a relief when the family socialising was over. Her aunt drove her to the airport to catch her three-thirty flight to Melbourne. Beth made the effort to say what she felt needed saying.

"I'm sorry it didn't work out, Aunty Em. I know you must be disappointed."

"Not to worry, dear," came the quick and kind assurance. "It would have been nice to have Tom close, but I'm really quite happy in my granny flat at Martin's. And there's no harm done, since Tom didn't know about the auction, anyway." Determinedly looking on the bright side.

Beth wished she could see a bright side. She'd been in a trough of dark despondency ever since she'd locked herself in her hotel room yesterday evening.

They stopped at a traffic light, and her aunt threw her a sharp and concerned scrutiny. "Are you all right, Beth?"

She managed a rueful smile. "I'll survive. Just a bit bruised at the moment."

Her aunt nodded sympathetically. "It's hard to let go. I hoped.... Well, never mind. Water under the bridge now."

The traffic light changed, and they were off again.

Beth knew what her aunt had hoped—that her niece would find what she wanted with Jamie. Perhaps the breakup with Gerald had triggered the thought, undoubtedly strengthened by Beth's impulse to see Jim Neilson at the gallery. The speculation had certainly been in her aunt's eyes after the auction yesterday. It would have been a nice, sentimental outcome on every level.

Beth had given it every chance, with a zero result. Worse than zero. Aunty Em was perceptive enough to close the door on it. There would be no more press clippings about Jim Neilson. What good could come of opening wounds?

"Well, it clears the decks for something else, doesn't it?" Beth remarked on a lighter note.

"Yes, it does," her aunt quickly agreed. "Best way to look at it."

The forced optimism closed the conversation. When the little Mazda pulled up outside the domestic terminal, there was a heavy sense of leave-taking. Their eyes ached with all the unspoken things.

"Take good care of yourself, Beth. And Tom."

"I will."

They hugged and kissed. Beth collected her luggage, then waved her aunt goodbye. Once inside the terminal she automatically went about the business of getting her seat allocation, then moving to the departure lounge. It was good to finally get on the plane and feel it lift off from Sydney. These past few days were really behind her now. She was in transit to another time and place.

During the flight, Beth tried to keep her mind turned to the future. She had the means to move herself and her father somewhere else, but where? Would any country property do? The lure of buying the old family farm had kept her from thinking of other options. She'd hoped to give her father an exciting surprise. Probably the most sensible course now was simply to discuss the future with him, try to arouse an interest in some new enterprise.

It didn't matter where she was. The only requirement for her writing was a personal computer and a printer. Her imagination went with her. No restrictions on that. With Gerald out of her life, she had no attachments in Melbourne, nothing to keep her there.

She'd never really had the time to make close friends—looking after her brothers and sisters, attending classes at night, studying in any spare hours she had. Then, in later years, Gerald, who had drawn her into mixing with a social circle that had been more his than hers. Somewhere along the line, she'd missed a boat other people took, and she didn't know how to change that. She knew she lived too much in her mind.

Perhaps it was the sense of apartness that had seeded the need for Jamie to still be there for her, regardless of the years that had passed. To her it had been a very special relationship. An ideal. Never achieved with anyone else. But she had probably idealised it beyond any reality.

She shrugged away her disillusionment as the plane landed at Tullamarine Airport. It didn't take her long to get to her car in the parking station. The drive home passed in a weary haze. As she heaved her luggage across the pavement to the iron gate that led into the terrace house where her family had lived for the past fifteen years, she couldn't help thinking how unimpressed Jim Neilson would be with it. Definitely low-life compared to his penthouse. But it still had more heart in it than his material luxury had.

She manoeuvred through the gateway, stepped on the porch and used her key to open the front door. No sooner had she pushed into the hallway than her father was calling, "Is that you, Beth?"

"Yes, Dad. Home safe and sound," she answered, shoving the door shut behind her.

To her surprise he came to the end of the hall from the living room, apparently stirred out of his usual apathy to welcome her home. His face was beaming with pleasure. He must have really missed her, Beth thought.

"Leave your bags. I'll carry them up later." He beckoned excitedly. "We've got a visitor." He laughed and shook his head. "You'll never guess who it is."

Whoever it was had certainly perked him up. Had her sister Kate flown home from London? Beth dropped her bags and hurried forward, her mind abuzz with happy anticipation. She needed a lift in spirits. If it was Kate...

Her father stood back and waved like a master conjuror working a gasp-worthy illusion. Beth was grinning as she stepped into the living room, her eyes delightedly seeking...

Jim Neilson?

Her skipping heart skidded to a dead halt. So did her feet. Her eyes glazed with shock. She felt the blood draining from her face, strength draining from her thighs. Her father was saying something, but his words were a vague buzz in her ears. Her mind registered only the booming reality of Jim Neilson standing by the table in the living room of her home. He was too magnetically solid to be a phantom of yesterday.

Her father flung an arm around her shoulders, hugging her with an exuberance that probably saved her from fainting. It jolted her into taking a deep breath, swallowing hard, fiercely willing the tremulous feeling to recede. Her mind clutched at what her father was saying, needing information.

"Not often Beth is knocked speechless." His tone was jovial, brimming with good humour. "It's like a bolt from the blue, your descending on us after all these years. You'll have to excuse her, Jim."

Jim! Very chummy. Plus complete ignorance of *Jim* having seen her yesterday and the day before.

Jim didn't correct him, either. He moved forward, hands lifting in charming appeal, white teeth flashing in a dazzling smile, dark eyes compelling compliance with his deceit. He was even dressed in sheep's clothing, smartly tailored navy trousers, a fashionable Fair Isle sweater in navy, dark red and deep green, a white shirt with a collar. Very conventional.

"Beth." A throb of sound, mesmerising in its expression of deep emotion. "You've grown into such a beautiful woman, you take my breath away."

Hardly, since he could speak with such glib ease.

She gave him a smouldering look that should have scorched him into nonexistence, but he kept coming at her with unshaken purpose.

Her father chuckled, delighted with her supposed effect on her childhood friend.

Jim Neilson had the unmitigated gall to take her hands, his fingers caressing her palms, making her skin tingle—no, crawl with revulsion. It had to be revulsion.

"Your father's been telling me all about you," he said, his tone full of warm admiration, his eyes boring into hers with challenging intensity. "How you took over your mother's role when you were only sixteen, what a great job you've done with your brothers and sisters, the long haul to getting your university degree. And making a wonderful success with your children's books. You are one amazing lady, Beth."

She found her tongue. "Oh, I think I could safely say you're more amazing."

Her eyes sizzled with outrage at his pumping her father for information about her behind her back. She extracted her hands and pointedly wiped them down the sides of the long tunic she wore over her comfortable travelling trousers, eradicating the disturbing sense of his touch. Her mind raced through a bank of words, seeking the most effective, the most telling, the most scathing terms she could use to cut his feet out from under him and show him up for the conscienceless cad he was.

"You don't know the half of it, Beth," her father crowed. "Jim saw that our old family farm was up for auction and he went and bought it. He says it's shamefully run down and he wants me to go into partnership with him to build it back up to what it should be. How about that!"

In one killing stroke, the urge to blow Jim Neilson's charade into blistering smithereens was hopelessly undermined. The wild energy burning up her brain lost its direction, totally subverted by red-light signals that forced it down other paths.

To destroy her father's joy without first investigating what had been said and done in her absence would not be a good thing. She wasn't the only person to be considered here. It was not in her character to dash anybody's dream, especially that of someone as dear to her as her father.

This had better be real. Her eyes flashed the message to Jim Neilson with fierce intent. If it was some manipulative game, she'd boil him in oil and feed him to pigs.

"Well, you've quite taken *my* breath away," she said, inhaling deeply, then sighing at length to cover the frenzied activity in her mind.

"Jim's got it all worked out," her father went on.

I bet he has, Beth thought venomously.

"Come and sit down, love. I'll get you a cup of coffee. You're probably dry from your flight," her father said with surprising consideration. "Then I'll tell you what the plan is."

"We've got so much to catch up on," Jim Neilson said eagerly, stepping back to draw out a chair from the table for her, showing gentlemanly courtesy to impress her father.

It didn't impress Beth one bit!

Nevertheless, she dutifully sat, hating the sense of him hovering behind her, her teeth gnashing in vampirish blood lust if he dared to touch her again.

"Like another coffee, Jim?" her father asked, collecting two empty mugs from the table.

"Yes, I would, thanks."

He moved out of the danger zone, to the chair he'd obviously occupied before Beth's arrival. The distance restored a modicum of control over the violent impulses he stirred in her. She studiously ignored him, noting what information was readily available about what had been going on here.

The mugs hadn't been the only objects littering the table. In front of her father's usual place were the sale papers from the auction. A plate of cake crumbs indicated that Jim Neilson had been enjoying hospitality for quite some time. More disturbing was the family photograph album, a pictorial history that had undoubtedly filled in some of the past fifteen years for him. Probably bored him out of his mind. Though it served him right for pretending an interest. The press clippings Aunty Em had sent were laid out for him, too, embarrassing evidence of their interest in him. Some of the children's books she'd written had also been proudly produced for display.

He picked one up. "I hope you don't mind. Your father said I could take these to read. I'd like to see what you've done, Beth."

From anyone else it would be a compliment. Her eyes derided his sincerity. "You're welcome. I have plenty of spare copies," she said, letting him know he wasn't taking anything irreplaceable from her. She waved at the mess on the table. "You must have been here for a while."

"Yes. A few hours."

"Did you have difficulty in finding us . . . after all these years?"

"No. No problem."

Beth seethed with anger. No problem once he set his mind to it. He'd probably got her address from the hotel. She put on a saccharine smile. "I'm surprised you remembered us."

"I never really forgot you, Beth." His eyes seared hers with very recent memories. "I guess you could say our lives took different turns."

"Yes. Very different," she mocked.

"I'd like to think the farm will bring us together again."

Not in a million years! "Well, you've certainly got Dad excited by it. What made you think of investing in land?"

"It's not so much an investment as a personal interest."

She gave him a look of wide-eyed wonder. "You mean you don't expect to make a profit out of it?"

A muscle in his cheek contracted, but he eyed her steadily. "Some things are more important than money."

Like great sex on tap... until it burns out? Or not being beaten?

"Why does this have importance to you?" she asked, determined to pin down his duplicity. "You turned your back on the valley fifteen years ago. Not even leaving a forwarding address."

"I didn't have an address, Beth," he said quietly. "I didn't stay any place for long. When I did finally get myself more established, so much time had gone by, there didn't seem much point—"

"What point is there now?" she cut in, relentlessly pursuing his purpose.

His dark eyes gleamed with intense determination. "A chance to find what was lost."

Mission impossible—on every count! She'd been there, done that and knew the outcome. There could be no changing it after yesterday's soul-emptying debacle.

"I told Jim about the letters you wrote, Beth," her father said, returning to the table with the coffee. "He said he never got them. Old Jorgen must have kept them, stingy old bastard. I explained you didn't write any more after you got the note from Mrs. Hutchens saying Jamie had gone and no one knew where he was."

But he'd known where she was. Known and hadn't cared. She'd given him their Melbourne address before they left the valley. No doubt he'd say he lost it with moving around so much. People on the way up had a habit of dropping baggage that wasn't useful to them any more. All he cared about was getting her into his bed at his convenience. Jim Neilson didn't lose what he wanted.

"Well, that's ancient history," she said, as if in light dismissal of an old grief that wasn't worth resurrecting. "Tell me about the plan for the farm, Dad."

He sat down, looking ten years younger than he had three days ago. He couldn't stop smiling, and his eyes sparkled with happiness. "It's very simple and straightforward, Beth. Jim's going to supply the finance and I'll supply the labour and management. I'm still as fit as a fiddle, so there's no problem there."

Years of labour in the Melbourne dockyards had certainly kept him strong physically. It had been his mental health worrying Beth. From the day he'd turned fifty-five and been retrenched from work, he seemed to have been willing himself to die, shuffling around in a deep depression, endlessly grieving over Kevin, finding no joy in anything.

The difference in him brought a lump to her throat. He looked almost spry, eager to get on with life. It was like a miracle. Though Beth found it bitterly ironic that Jim Neilson could take the credit for what she'd hoped to achieve. With *her* plan!

She focused her attention on the man currently in the box seat, wary of accepting anything at face value where he was concerned. Some cross-examination was definitely in order.

"Doesn't Dad have to put any money into this partnership?"

"No. There is a lot of work involved," he said with earnest appeal. "I'm afraid the house is a shambles. Practically everything's fallen into disrepair. Fences need replacing. It'll come as a shock to your father when he first sees it."

"Don't you worry about that, Jim. It'll be the prettiest sight I've seen in many a year," her father said with enthusiastic assurance.

It curdled Beth's stomach. If Jim Neilson was game-playing, it was getting very dirty. Beth hated the necessity of playing devil's advocate, but she had to protect her father. "Is this to be a legal partnership, drawn up properly?"

"Absolutely," Jim Neilson said firmly.

"I wouldn't like Dad to uproot his life here if you're likely to change your mind in a month or two. An impulsive whim can come and go," she warned meaningfully. "And sometimes people don't get the result they want," she added for good measure.

"Point taken, Beth," he said, his eyes meeting the challenge in hers with every appearance of unshakable equanimity. "I won't change my mind. I know what the farm means to your father and I know what it means to me. I'll be instructing my solicitor on the partnership tomorrow. And I'll have it put in my will that if I predecease your father, he will inherit my half of the property, giving him sole ownership."

She was taken aback by such a final settlement. And his total lack of any hesitation. Resolution was written on his face, and she started to wonder if he was acting from a sense of guilt rather than headstrong desire.

"That's very generous of you," she said tentatively.

"I think it only fair... in the circumstances."

He had certainly done her a few injustices. Was this his way of making restitution? He had admitted feeling guilty yesterday morning, before he'd soothed his conscience with the rotten assumptions he'd made. When she'd comprehensively smashed them, perhaps the guilt had really come home to roost. Even so, to act on it to this extent seemed incredibly extravagant. Though it was in keeping with the fast decisiveness Beth had come to associate with him.

"I wouldn't expect your father to move until all the legalities are completed," he went on, clearing her doubts about the extraordinary deal.

"Your solicitor can check that everything is bona fide. Please feel free to question any part of the agreement. It won't go ahead until you're satisfied."

"We've talked it all through, Beth," her father said confidently. "Jim's going to put a caravan on the property to begin with. It'll give us a place to live until I get the house shipshape again."

Beth raised her eyebrows incredulously at Jim Neilson. "You're going to live there, too?"

"No, no," her father corrected, laughing. "It's for you and me, Beth. Jim's too tied up with his business to be on hand. That's why he needs me."

"I see," she murmured, dropping her lashes to veil the recoil in her eyes.

She could feel her face tightening. They were both assuming she'd accompany her father. While Jim Neilson might not be on hand, she would be...to a frequent visitor. Her father's partner had every right to come to the farm whenever he liked.

It burst through her mind that this partnership had nothing to do with guilt, nothing to do with generosity, nothing to do with any sentimentality over rebuilding what had been laid waste, nothing to do with her father or the farm at all. It had to do with making her readily accessible to Jim Neilson.

A chance to find what was lost.

She'd walked out on him and what he'd offered, and he wanted another chance at getting her where he wanted her. This was simply a different approach, a clever manipulation, going through her father to seal the situation, counting on daughterly love for compliance. In Jim Neilson's own words, psychologically brilliant. Except she didn't have to play.

"Is there some problem, Beth?"

The anxious note in her father's voice begged her not to spoil his rosy dream. But she had a life, too, and she'd given up much of it for the sake of her family. For her the past was gone. No point in revisiting it. No heart for it, either.

She reached out and squeezed her father's hand, her eyes pleading for his understanding. "I'm delighted for you, Dad. I guess it feels right to you, and I'm truly glad about that. I'm not so sure it's right for me."

He frowned, unable to imagine what reservations she might have. "Why not?"

She had no intention of discussing her personal feelings in front of Jim Neilson. "Let me think about it. Okay?" She offered an appeasing smile. "You have rather landed this on me."

"I just thought..."

He looked from her to Jim Neilson, and she knew he was thinking Jamie, not Jim—Jamie and Beth as it used to be. And her heart cried for what had been truly lost.

"I think it best I go now so you can discuss this between yourselves," Jim Neilson put in smoothly, acting the sensitive soul to perfection.

"No, no," her father protested. "You must stay for dinner, Jim. I'm sure Beth—"

"Actually I wanted to ask Beth if she'd have dinner with me tonight," he cut in even more smoothly, a note of warm appeal in his voice.

"Oh! Oh, yes! What a good idea!" her father cried. "You'd love that, Beth, wouldn't you?" he pressed eagerly. No prizes for being a subtle matchmaker!

No way was she going to put herself in a position where the wolf could eat her again! All the same, there was a certain perverse pleasure in punching home that point. "What do you have in mind for dinner, Jim?" she asked in a light lilt, her eyes aglow with a tigerish gleam.

"There's a very fine restaurant, Marchetti's Latin, in Lonsdale Street. I'd like to take you there," he answered as though he was completely on the level, no devious plans at all for sex on the side. Or as the main course!

Marchetti's Latin was reputed to be one of the classiest restaurants in Melbourne, renowned for its ambience, service and food. He was obviously laying out the red carpet to tempt her. And, in fact, he owed her for the bogus dinner invitation he'd given her at the gallery on Friday night. Not that she wanted to even some petty score with him.

Nevertheless, maybe she should not smack him down too soon. It could be worthwhile to take this opportunity to speak to Jim Neilson without her father listening. Best he be left in no doubt where she stood on this partnership deal. It did not involve her. If that meant Jim Neilson backing out of it, better now than later for letting her father down.

"How lovely!" she said, smiling sweetly. "I'd be very happy to meet you there at eight o'clock. Does that suit?"

"I hired a car. I can easily pick you up and bring you home, Beth."

Any car with him in it was a keg of dynamite. "It would be bringing you out of your way twice to fetch me here and back. Thank you, but I prefer to drive my own car." *And stay in control of where and when I go.* Her eyes flashed the message to him.

"As you wish," he conceded.

He had no choice. Beth had no intention of giving him one after the power-game tricks he'd played on her.

"Independent women," her father muttered disapprovingly.

Jim Neilson grinned at him. "Beth never did like to be helped. She was one feisty little girl."

She would have kicked him under the table if he hadn't been rising from it, pushing his chair back, ready to take his leave. If he remembered that about her, why had he assumed she'd come to him for help with money? A bit of inconsistency there, Mr. Neilson, she thought bitingly.

Nevertheless, her father's good humour was restored by the deft stroke of old memories. He was chuckling as he rose from his chair to see his guest out. Good manners pushed Beth into standing, too, although she pointedly stayed by her chair. Jim Neilson paused, taking in her stiff stance, realising she would not accompany him to the door.

"Until tonight," she said briefly, her eyes flat, promising nothing.

He nodded slowly, his eyes kindling with a dark fire that promised a furnace of feeling. "Until tonight," he repeated.

Unreasonably, unaccountably, despite the hardest defences against him, those two words thudded into Beth's heart, and she knew it wouldn't matter what precautions she took. Jim Neilson would always be dangerous.

CHAPTER TWELVE

BETH dressed to kill. Why not? Opportunities to wear the outfit she'd bought for her youngest sister's wedding were rare. Marchetti's Latin certainly rated the best she had in her wardrobe. Besides, female vanity insisted she carry off this last night with Jim Neilson in style, so much style he would choke on it.

The silverstone-cut velvet evening jacket was a masterpiece of sensual elegance. The sweetheart neckline dipped into a row of covered buttons fastened by loops that kept the bodice snugly moulded to her breasts and waist. The long sleeves were slightly flared to match the swing of the jacket over her hips. Her skirt, in contrast, was sheer feminine frivolity, a peppermint silk georgette waterfall style that frothed around her thighs, leaving a long expanse of leg in pale silk tights. Her high-heeled white sandals crisscrossed her feet with thin straps, finally fastening above her ankles.

Her make-up was immaculate. Red lipstick, red fingernails. She'd washed and blow-dried her hair into a smooth, shining mane that swished around her shoulders. A spray of Christian Dior Poison on her pulse points and she was ready to fire on all cylinders.

When she went downstairs to bid her father good night, her glamorous appearance put the twinkle in his eyes. "Going to knock him dead?" he teased.

"I'm not a little girl any more," she reminded him.

"Ah!" he said, as though her reluctance to commit herself to country life with him was now answered. With a little smirk that suggested he understood how the wind was blowing, he added, "Well, I think Jim will do you proud, Beth."

"Time will tell," she said dryly. "Don't wait up for me, Dad."

"You go right ahead and enjoy yourself," he said benevolently. "I'll be off to bed soon. Had enough excitement for one day."

Beth hoped it was not about to turn sour on him.

As she drove to Lonsdale Street, she seriously pondered the position Jim Neilson had taken. He might be something of a shark on the money market, but she shied from believing he lacked all integrity. Her father was a complete innocent in what had developed as a highly personal and private battle of wills between them. To brush him aside as a dispensable casualty after dragging him into the fray would be utterly contemptible.

Jim Neilson had judged her contemptibly, but he had no reason to treat her father the same way. In hindsight, and with a much cooler head, Beth had to concede she had acted, well, rashly, in trying to find Jamie in Jim Neilson. Even recklessly. But she didn't want her father to be a victim of her foolish pursuit of a dream. It wouldn't be fair.

Not that life was fair. It wasn't fair that Jamie had been dumped on a grandfather like old Jorgen. It wasn't fair that her mother had died so young. It wasn't fair that her father had been burdened with so many griefs. Was Jim Neilson so ruthless he would hurt an older man who'd never done him any harm? Was he so callous he only saw her father as a means to a totally selfish end?

Well, she would soon have the answers, Beth thought with a wave of determination. No fencing tonight. It was all cards on the table, face up.

Since it was Sunday night, she had no trouble parking on Lonsdale Street, and she didn't even have to feed coins into a meter. She was glad of her velvet jacket on the short walk from the car to the restaurant. The nip in the air was a sharp reminder that early spring was much colder in Melbourne than in Sydney. She would probably feel a lot colder, in every sense, when she emerged from the restaurant after this showdown.

The building that housed the restaurant brought a smile. It was small, old and painted green, a brave statement of lasting individuality amongst the skyscrapers that surrounded it right here in the centre of the city. Double glass doors formed the entrance. She checked her watch. It was still a few minutes to eight. Uncaring whether Jim Neilson was punctual or not, she opened the door, stepped inside and was immediately enveloped in an atmosphere of old-world elegance.

The maître d' was on the spot to greet her, gracious and charming. No sooner did she mention Jim Neilson than she was addressed by name. "Ah, yes, Miss Delaney—" an admiring smile "—Mr. Neilson is waiting for you at the bar. If you'll come this way?"

The moment she saw him her surroundings blurred. He was on watch for her arrival, his gaze trained on her every step towards him, generating instant heat. He looked so damned imposing, impressive, dynamically sexy in a sleek black dinner suit teamed with the unconventional note of a white silk polo-necked shirt.

Beth deliberately distracted herself by looking at the magnificent floral arrangement adorning the bar. Though if anyone had asked her afterwards what flowers were used to create it, she wouldn't have been able to name one of them. She was too intensely aware of feeling naked.

Worse than naked. Her mind somehow reproduced the sensation of his mouth tugging on her breasts, his thighs lying between hers, the power of him surging into her. Her muscles contracted, reliving the intense pleasure of that savage intimacy.

He stood to greet her. He didn't offer his hand or try to take hers. When she deigned to meet his gaze, she had the strong impression he was just as intensely engaged in mentally measuring the physical impact she had on him. The maître d' eased the electric tension by offering her a glass of champagne with his compliments. She thanked him and tried to relax, taking the bar stool offered.

Jim Neilson resumed his seat as they were discreetly left to converse alone. A wry smile tilted his mouth. "It's not working," he murmured.

Beth lifted a mocking eyebrow. "Your master plan?"

He shook his head. "You wear the colours of winter frost. I feel the heat of high summer."

She gestured to the martini on the marble-topped bar beside him. "Perhaps you should ask for some ice in your drink. It might cool your temperature if you're uncomfortable."

He laughed. "You always were quick with words. I enjoyed reading your books, Beth. You have a real talent for storytelling."

It surprised her that he'd bothered to read the ones he'd taken. Was his interest genuine or contrived? "Which did you like best?" she tested.

"The one about the snake," he answered, grinning with the touch of boyishness she found unsettling. "It instantly reminded me of our experience up at the old quarry. Brought it all back to me. You were very brave that day, Beth." His eyes caressed her with glowing admiration. "I didn't think a girl would have so much guts."

She frowned, not wanting him to tap into their childhood together. Not now. She sipped the champagne as she sought to take the initiative from him. "The books are doing very well.

They've been sold to Britain and the U.S., so their popularity is building," she stated matter-of-factly.

"That's great!" he declared.

"It's useful," she corrected tersely, not wanting her ego stroked. Her eyes flashed a flat rejection of the warmth he was projecting as she established the important point. "I can afford to buy Dad's partnership in the farm."

His mouth twisted. "I wasn't aware it was for sale."

She ignored the remark, boring straight to the business end of the deal she could offer. "Eventually I hope my income will provide the means to buy you out if you're prepared to wait a while."

"Thus severing all connection with me," he drawled.

"At least it's honest," she snapped. "I'm not trying to get something else on the side."

"I don't want your money, Beth."

"I know perfectly well what you *want*," she said angrily, then tried to lower her temperature by drinking the cold champagne.

"And I'll lay odds your father doesn't want you to use it on him," came the rather sobering judgment. "He's a proud man."

It troubled her, that thought. She hadn't been considering her father's reaction to the safeguard she was trying to put into place, only the need to remove any obligation to Jim Neilson. She watched him sip his martini, resenting the knowing authority with which he had spoken, yet unable to dismiss the doubt it had put in her mind.

"You haven't discussed this with him, have you?" he said, more in the tone of a statement than a question.

She didn't answer, brooding over her drink.

"He wouldn't have liked you buying the farm for him, either. It would have made him feel more of a failure, Beth," he went on quietly. "I know you had the best of intentions, wanting to help, wanting to give him a reason to get out of bed in the morning."

She looked at him with pained eyes. How could he understand so much in so little time?

"It's better coming from me than from you, Beth. He can take pride in acting for me, doing what I can't. If you had offered it..." He shook his head. "Your father feels he owes you too much already. It's one of the burdens he feels most keenly."

"He doesn't owe me," she protested.

"I listened to him all afternoon."

"You had no right to—to..."

"To listen?"

"Under false pretences of caring," she accused bitterly.

His eyes held hers in steady challenge. "You denied me the chance to listen, Beth. Denied me the chance of caring. Why are you angry because your father opened up to me?"

"Oh, I don't suppose the timing has anything to do with it," she mocked.

"Perhaps it never felt right to me to intrude on your life. Until now."

"And now it feels right?"

"Yes. It does."

"Not to me, it doesn't."

"I know. And I hope to correct that."

"Well, that should be a good trick." She drained her glass and set it down. "Do start," she invited derisively.

He stood up, not bothering to finish his martini. He caught the eye of the maître d', who instantly responded, coming over to escort them to their table. Beth slid off her bar stool, ready to accompany him, coolly keeping distance between them so as not to allow even the accidental brushing of hands. He could talk himself blue in the face, she thought, and he still wouldn't win her over. Physical contact wasn't going to work for him, either.

Despite its being a Sunday night, the restaurant was well patronised. Beth was acutely aware of the attention they drew from other diners. The women, of course, were looking at Jim Neilson. Most of the men did, too. He had such a commanding presence, to say the least. She was measured up as his partner. Beth didn't care if she did him credit or not.

Her interest was captured by the marvellous brass gondola that took centre stage in the dining room. It was about a metre long and was mounted on a glass stand propped by two cyprus trees in brass. It was enough to transport anyone to another time and place, redolent of the riches of Venice at the height of its power.

They were led to an intimate table for two, positioned against the centre of the wall on the right-hand side of the restaurant where a huge mirror towered up to the tall ceiling. A glance around convinced Beth it was the best table in the restaurant. And they were certainly getting VIP service, the maître d' seeing them comfortably seated, introducing them to the waiter who would look after them for the evening, listing the chef's specialties he personally recommended.

The food sounded divine, and Beth decided immediately she would have the mud crab pasta— tortellini filled with Queensland mud crab and served with butter and chive sauce—followed by the crisp duck—half a duckling boned and roasted and served with lemon peppercorn sauce—followed, if she could fit it in, by the chocolate and coffee soufflé. There was no point in not enjoying what she could of this experience with Jim Neilson.

He chose the ravioli, filled with pumpkin and dried fruit and almonds, which also sounded delicious, then decided on seafood for his main course, the filleted barramundi. A consultation with the wine waiter resulted in the selection of an Italian white wine, Bollini chardonnay, and a Mount Mary Australian red. Beth reminded herself to have only a glass of each since she was driving, but she certainly wanted to taste everything that was on offer in this fabulous place.

A small plate of appetisers was already on the table, oysters and delectable little savouries to tempt their appetite. As she nibbled on one of the latter, she deliberately avoided another immediate confrontation with Jim Neilson, casting her gaze around all the noteworthy features of the decor. The ambience was too special not to savour while she was here. She would probably never come again.

One very grand painting in a glorious gilt frame caught her eye. It depicted one of Henry the Eighth's weddings.

''Do you like it?''

The waiters had gone. Beth mentally braced herself to face the man who was paying for all this. Handsomely, no doubt. Though whatever the cost, it was not going to buy what he wanted.

''To what are you referring?'' she asked coolly, knowing she had to be warily sifting whatever he said and did this evening. She was not about to fall for any tricks he had up his sleeve.

''The painting.'' His smile was disarming, full of whimsical charm.

Beth hastily erected defences, glancing at Henry's wedding. ''It seems to be slightly out of focus or something.''

''The artist's style. It's a Philip Barker.''

She supposed art collecting had familiarised him with many well-known names. Then another thought struck her. "You've been here before."

"Yes," he admitted, meeting the accusation in her eyes without any apparent concern.

"But that wasn't the right time to pay us a visit," she mocked.

"I imagined you married. With children."

"Easy enough to call and find out."

"No. It wasn't easy, Beth. I don't expect you to understand, but there was a barrier I couldn't cross. I would never have crossed it but for you coming to me . . . and breaking it down."

He sounded sincere. He looked sincere. Beth refused to believe it. Her silence scorned his convenient, self-made barrier.

He leaned back in his chair, regarding her thoughtfully. Beth sensed his mind wandering down various tracks, searching for the most effective way to reach out to her. It was rather ironic, considering how desperately she'd tried to do the same with him only two nights ago.

"When I first saw you in the gallery," he said slowly, startling her by coming in on the same time frame as her own thoughts, "I couldn't take my eyes off you. You made me think of spring. You looked so fresh and appealing. It warmed something in me. I wanted to know you. I asked Claud who you were."

"Claud?" It came out harshly, like a squawk. The quiet intensity of Jim Neilson's words had somehow seized her by the throat.

"The owner of the gallery. He was surprised. He thought I knew." A wry smile curled his lips. "After all, you'd given my name to the attendant at the door, in lieu of a formal invitation."

A flush seared her cheeks. He'd known she'd lied to get in, using his name as a passport. Known before he'd approached her. Which put a different complexion on his subsequent actions. "What did you think?" she blurted.

He shrugged. "Some women will do anything to get to a man they fancy. It's happened to me a few times." He grimaced with distaste. "Usually I cut them dead."

The heat grew painful. "Why not me?"

"I was angry. It spoiled the image I'd been building in my mind. Spoiled the feeling. I wanted to punish you for looking so attractive and being so deceptive."

"I see," she muttered, her whole body clenching at the realisation of what had been simmering underneath his surface that night.

"And the worst of it was, no matter what I told myself, the attraction was still there. And I gave in to it, even as I fought it."

Hating her, hating himself. No wonder it had been impossible to crack those barriers. The seething sense of barely repressed violence came back to her. That was what had ignited the same feelings in her, the fierce passion she had never experienced before. Hating him, hating herself. Yet unable to let go.

The wine waiter returned with the chilled chardonnay. It was a welcome diversion. While Jim Neilson tasted and approved the wine, Beth managed to regain her composure and her wits. There was no denying a strong attraction between them. That didn't excuse Jim Neilson's way of pursuing it after he knew who she was, especially using the old family farm as a lever to get what he wanted from her. She *could* let go now. She was determined never to see him again after tonight.

Having poured the wine into their glasses and placed the bottle in a nearby ice bucket, the waiter left. Beth took a small sip of the cool liquid. Her throat was very dry.

"Why didn't you tell me who you were, Beth? Right there in the gallery when I asked you."

"I only came to see you," she answered in defence. "I used your name because I didn't know how else to get in. I just wanted to see what you were like now."

"But when I came to you..."

"You didn't recognise me," she accused hotly, uncaring how unreasonable that might be. Somehow he should have known—if there'd been anything of Jamie left in him.

"Maybe I did, Beth, on some subconscious level," he said softly, his eyes piercing hers with such deep intensity, she felt them boring into her soul. "Maybe that was the attraction I felt, beyond any ordinary common sense. Telling me you were uniquely special in some very meaningful way."

"Stop it!" she returned, angry that he was tugging at her so powerfully. "You're just trying to seduce me with lies now."

"Am I? How else can I explain what I did when I've never done anything like it before?"

"Why not put it down to good, old-fashioned lust?"

"Because it was more than that. And you know it, Beth."

"That's all I felt coming from you, Jim Neilson, and God knows I wanted more," she retorted fiercely, hating the confusion he stirred in her, rejecting it in favour of what she knew with certainty.

He leaned forward, eyes blazing with passion, voice throbbing with conviction. "You would have had more. Much more. If you'd only told me who you were right then and there."

She recoiled from him, bristling with pride. Her hands clenched in her lap, fists wanting to pummel him for his rotten, insidious lies. "You didn't want to know me. I would only have been a reminder of the valley you'd left behind. The life you hated."

"Then why am I here, Beth? Why have I just tied myself to the valley again?"

"You told me why." She hurled the words at him. "So you can keep laying me until the fire's burned out."

"I wanted more of you, damn it!" He leaned forward, his eyes stabbing hers with a ferocity of soul that was prepared to smash anything in his path. "The fact that I didn't care what it cost me—and I'm talking more than money here—should give you some idea of how deeply you'd got to me. And if you think I'd pay that much for sex—however great—you're crazy."

He jabbed a finger at her. "It was you...you who limited us to a sexual connection. And that was so explosive there had to be more behind it. But you gave me nothing else to work with. Not a damned thing about where you were coming from."

His mouth thinned. He made a slashing gesture. "I worked with what you gave me. What you led me to believe. And if you're honest with yourself, Beth Delaney, you'll damned well admit it instead of sitting on some high moral stand, pretending you didn't ride with me down the road we took. For whatever reason you did it, you came with me every step of the way."

His eyes dared her to deny it.

She couldn't.

"So I called it wrong," he went on. "Big crime. Never mind how much you'd misled me with your actions. Now you consider it another crime that I came and found out what your life has been like since you left the valley. The truth of the matter is you could have told me on Friday night what your father told me today. And it would have saved all this—'' his mouth twisted in savage feeling ''—this hell.''

''And you could have come to Melbourne and found out for yourself years ago. Years ago, Jim Neilson,'' she repeated with the fury of her pent-up passion.

All his justifications were fair enough, she had to concede, looking from his point of view. But she had a point of view, too! He'd betrayed her faith in something so rare—soul mates, always and forever...she'd been so certain of it. A child's certainty, she corrected with bitter cynicism.

He closed his eyes, shook his head as though deeply pained by her reminder of a truth he didn't want to look at. He dragged in a deep breath, opened his eyes and settled in his chair as he slowly exhaled. His face was set in lines of hard pride. He gave her a look of dark derision.

''I came. I came when I was eighteen. I saw you step out of your home with a fold-up pram and a baby in your arms.''

Kevin.

Except he hadn't known about Kevin.

Nor about her mother dying.

''And I said to myself, Jamie, my boy, she didn't wait for you. You've been living in a dream. So I went back to Sydney and pursued a different dream.''

Those few blunt facts, tossed at her in an offhand drawl, completely shattered her case against him. Beth sat in stunned silence, trying to absorb the shock, the awful realisation of his disappointment and disillusionment, however falsely based it was.

He had come, as he said he would, as she had believed he would. Not for one moment did she think this was a lie. It rang true. The bond they had shared, so deep, so special. They'd sworn that time and distance would not diminish it. And he thought she had betrayed it, giving herself to another in an intimacy that should have been unthinkable in the span of time before he came. When he was eighteen.

She *had* been waiting for him, waiting for many more years before hope and faith were whittled away. If only he'd come up to her, spoken to her...

"If you want to blame me for that, go ahead," he invited sardonically, as though tuned straight into her mind. "I know now I was wrong in what I thought. But nothing either you or I can say will change the past, Beth. Or change the years that have passed since then, what we made of them, what they made of us."

She couldn't speak, too shattered by the turn of fate that had killed off Jamie and created Jim Neilson. Mourning was not going to restore what had been irretrievably lost. And he was right about the effect of the long passage of years, far more years than they had spent together. They were no longer the children whose trust in each other had been absolute.

Blame was a pointless word. They had both reacted to unfulfilled dreams. Did he bear any more guilt than she in the way they had made their decisions?

"All we have is now, Beth," he said quietly. "And what we make of *now* will be the test of what we really feel about each other."

The waiter arrived with their entrees. Beth stared at her mud crab pasta. She knew she had to pick up a fork and start eating it. It would be a dreadful waste if she didn't. It looked superb. It smelled as inviting as it looked.

Yet her hands did not cooperate with what her senses were signalling. Her mind was jammed, twirling around the reality that had to be faced. Jamie *had* come. And gone. The sense of betrayal went both ways. They were both wrong. Which left her with *now*.

Did she want to lose what might be with Jim Neilson, given a fair chance?

CHAPTER THIRTEEN

I HAVE to deal with now.

Beth clutched that concept with painful intensity.

She picked up her fork. *Now* was the food in front of her. *Now* was Jim Neilson sitting across the table from her, a man who'd travelled alone to his mountain top, a man who'd left the ideals of his youth behind.

He picked up his fork. Her gaze was drawn to his long, lean fingers. They'd touched her with lust, not love. Did he have the capacity to love or was it gone? Did it matter now? Did anything matter now?

Deeply depressed, her heart aching for what had been lost, Beth speared a small envelope of pasta and lifted it to her mouth. Concentrate on taste, she told herself. Yes... There was the delicate flavour of mud crab. The butter and chive sauce was just right with it. The chef certainly knew how to produce a culinary masterpiece. This dish would surely satisfy any gourmet.

"Good?"

She looked up to see dark eyes sharply scanning hers, wanting, appealing for a response. To more than a question about her entree, Beth thought.

"Yes. Very good," she answered, warily choosing superficial politeness. "Yours?"

"A tantalising taste. It has a sweet and dry finish. Like to try some?"

He pushed his plate of ravioli closer to her, inviting her to share his experience. She hesitated. It was a friendly thing to do. Like smoking a peace pipe. Did she have any reason to hold onto her hostility towards him? She felt confused, stressed by emotions she hadn't sorted out yet.

He gave her a whimsical smile. "You always shared your school lunches with me. Can't I return the favour?"

For one sharp moment, she saw him on his first day at school, hauled there by Mrs. Hutchens against old Jorgen's will. When lunchtime came he'd sat alone on the big stump in the playground, a misfit amongst children who were used to the routine of school life. He had nothing to eat. He never did have anything to eat for lunch.

She'd braved the teasing she knew would follow and sat on the stump with him, asking him if he'd finish her lunch for her. Her mother was trying to fatten her up, but it was simply too much to eat, and if she took it home she'd get into trouble. Even then he'd been proud, not liking to take charity from anyone. But he'd succumbed to her five-year-old, little-girl guile and helped her out of a scolding from her mother.

Seven and five. They were now thirty and twenty-eight. Innocence gone. Trust gone. Faith gone. But it would be churlish not to accept the return of a favour.

She took a piece of his ravioli.

"Would you like some of mine?" she offered impulsively. "It's superb."

"Thanks, I will."

His smile grew warmer, a glow of pleasure in his eyes. It jiggled her heart, lifting it, making it pump faster. Her taste buds were suddenly more acute. She ate with relish, mentally shying away from examining what was happening to her or fighting against it. Somewhere in the back of her mind she knew it was impossible to return to the past. But it had been good in those days. No harm in remembering, was there?

Or was Jim Neilson manipulating those memories? If she separated him from Jamie—and she had to—what did she know about him? Hard, cynical, incisive, ruthless. A lone wolf. Sexy. Knowingly sexy. Aware and confident of his power to attract, both physically and in the challenge innate in the position he had attained. Alpha male on top of the mountain.

She was not immune to him.

He could hurt her. Badly.

She wanted Jamie back. He knew it and could use it to manoeuvre her into giving him what he wanted. The question was . . . what was the *much more* he wanted?

Could she meet it? Or would they both end up dissatisfied?

They emptied their plates, and the waiter took them away. They sipped the wine, content to let the issues between them rest for a while.

"You were never too thin, Beth."

She lifted her gaze and found the same old memories swimming in his eyes.

"You were always perfect to me," he added, his mouth soft and sensual in warm reminiscence.

She remembered how he had kissed her on the creek bank, the tantalising caress of his lips on hers, drawing her into that manic explosion of passion. How long could that be sustained? Would it be different now they knew more about each other?

"You've grown into a very beautiful woman."

Well, he'd certainly seen all of her. Felt all of her. And there was more than warmth in his eyes now. Heat, desire, simmering, arousing feelings she had great difficulty in suppressing. He was an exciting lover. Or rather a superb sexual athlete. With a body that incited lust.

Why give it up without trying for more? He wanted it. She wanted it, too, if she was honest with herself. But other things were more important. He might think her beautiful, but she certainly wasn't perfect. If she had to accept him as the person he was now, he had to accept the present-day Beth.

"I've recently broken up with a man I might have married," she blurted.

Desire was cooled with weighing speculation. It made her wonder if the recounting of a previous lover made her less desirable. But he had to have realised she was not inexperienced.

"Why didn't you marry him?"

It was a reasonable question. "Because..." *Because he wasn't you.* She frowned over the automatic response. The dream had not been rooted out. Its tentacles still clung to her heart.

"I haven't married either, Beth," he said quietly, not waiting for her reply. "I've had a number of relationships, but none of them measured up to what I wanted. What I'd once known."

"You said it was gone," she answered, letting him know any game-playing on that issue was in very bad taste.

His eyes locked onto hers, deeply challenging. "Has it?"

I don't know. She rushed into speech to cover the misery of not being sure of where she was going now. "I met Gerald at university. He's a lecturer. I was a mature-age student and he took an interest in me. It was good for a while."

"You enjoyed academia?"

"It was a larger world than I'd had up to that point. The people I met seemed to know a lot."

"Seemed?"

"It all came out of books. The *right* books."

He looked amused. "Are there wrong books?"

She grimaced. "Gerald referred to what I wrote as 'Beth's little children's books.'"

"Condescending. And probably jealous of your success. Did he have ambitions to get published himself?"

"He'd had some poems published. They were...very literary. Not easy to understand." She shrugged and shook her head. "I don't know why I'm talking about him. You can't want to know."

"You're wondering if I'd respect what you do...or belittle it."

She stared at him. Could he read her better than she did herself? In a way he was right. How would Jim Neilson behave towards her work?

"You've always been a giver, Beth," he went on, his voice softening to an intimate caress. "You gave to me from the first day we met. You gave to your family to hold it together when your father could not afford other help. You would have given him his farm. You're constantly giving to all the children who are entertained by your stories. I value that in you far too much to ever slight any part of it."

Strange. She'd never thought of herself in those terms. She liked to make people happy. It gave her pleasure. She wasn't as unselfish as Jamie...Jim made her out to be. Maybe this was a ruse to soften her up for a seduction scene. She looked hard at him, trying to probe what was really in his heart.

He grimaced. "You must be thinking I'm a taker. I certainly took all I could get from you when I was a boy. And this past weekend, I took

even more from you, justifying it with a lot of
false assumptions. When your father laid out the
reality of your life this afternoon—'' his eyes
begged her forgiveness ''—it was all so true of
the Beth you'd been to me, I was ashamed of
ever having imagined anything else.''

She had played her part in giving him a false
impression, Beth thought guiltily, allowing him—
a supposed stranger—to pick her up and carry
her off.

The tantalising question was, how much of Jim
Neilson was still true to the Jamie he'd been to
her? Pride, she thought. Not showing his hurts.
Determinedly rising above them. He'd always
shrugged off old Jorgen's beatings, giving other
excuses for his bruises, but she had known.
Known he had suffered for sneaking off to be
with her.

''I realise now you had it a lot harder than I
did,'' he murmured.

''No,'' she swiftly corrected. The stark lone-
liness in the painting hanging in his penthouse
living room was imprinted on her mind. The Brett
Whitely one, too, the scream of the soul. ''I
always had the love of my family around me.''

A wry look. ''Much better than material
possessions.''

Jamie had loved being with her family. Did he
still hanker for that warmth? ''You did wonder-
fully well for yourself. Got what you aimed for,''
she surmised. It was certainly no mean feat,
coming from nothing. ''You have every reason

to be proud of your successes. And take satisfaction from them."

"I won't pretend I don't. I like the rewards for what I've put in. But..."

He leaned forward and reached across the table, taking the hand she'd rested near her glass of wine, enveloping it with pressing warmth, his flesh making hers tingle. Her pulse took a megaleap. Her eyes flew to his, afraid of what advantage he meant to pursue, feeling more vulnerable to him now than ever before.

"Let me give, Beth," he pleaded with urgent intensity. "I want to give your father the farm. I want to give you whatever you'd like. Whatever would make you happy." He suddenly grinned. "Remember how much we wanted to see a circus? I still haven't been to one. Have you?"

She laughed out of sheer nervousness.

"Oh, I know that's trivial," he rushed on, his expression changing with bewildering speed, sobering to deep seriousness. "I know there are things I can't make up for. No one can." His fingers fondled caringly. "Like Kevin. I'm sorry he died, Beth. Bringing him up as you did, like a child of your own, it must have hurt so badly, losing him like that."

Tears welled into her eyes. "I gave him the bike for Christmas," she blurted, drawn by his sympathetic understanding to unburden her private grief. "I made him wait until he was ten. I thought he'd be sensible enough to ride it safely by then."

"It wasn't your fault. It was just an accident."

"I know. Dad blames the city. Sorry, I . . ."

She snatched her hand out of his and grabbed her handbag, quickly fumbling through it for a tissue. Her mascara would start running any second if she didn't mop up the damage and get herself under control. She was an emotional mess, being tugged in all directions, too many what ifs crowding in on her.

It was a relief when Jim Neilson drew his hand back to his glass. His physical effect on her was in no way abated. If anything, the connection to Jamie had increased it. She was hopelessly quivery inside. She barely managed to paste some composure on her face as she put the tissue away and set her bag beside her chair.

Fortunately she was given a breather with the arrival of their main course. The filleting of the barramundi was done right at their table, the waiter demonstrating admirable skill in deftly removing the fish from its bones. It was a welcome distraction for Beth. She didn't have to look at Jim Neilson for quite some time.

Once the waiter had departed, they started eating without resuming any conversation. Beth was gradually able to relax and enjoy her crisp duck with the lemon peppercorn sauce. The chef had definitely excelled himself.

"I'm glad I didn't spoil your appetite."

The rueful remark elicited a wry response. "That would have been a shame. This is heavenly food."

"Good to know I got something right."

He had achieved more than Beth could ever have anticipated, eroding her prejudice against him on so many levels she was in danger of forgetting all the negatives she had stacked up to protect herself from succumbing to the attraction that ran so strongly between them. In a way, they had been answered or explained. She found herself excusing his actions. And his non-actions. For the most part.

"Your father said Chris has joined the navy."

Of course he'd remember the brother closest to her in age. Chris had often tagged along with her and Jamie on their adventures. "Yes. He's sailing the Pacific at the moment."

"His uncle's influence?"

He obviously hadn't forgotten about her mother's brother fixing up a job for her father on the docks. And a low-rental house for them. It was why they had moved to Melbourne. Uncle Ray had been a merchant seaman, but Beth felt Chris had made up his own mind about his career choice.

"I think it was more to ease the financial situation at home," she answered. "Chris could continue an education in the navy. They paid for it."

"Of course."

"And it's a secure career."

"Some scars run deep, don't they?" he murmured sympathetically.

She wondered how deeply his scars ran. She knew that none of her family would ever forget the effect of bankruptcy on their father. On them, too. "It strikes people different ways. I think my sister Kate will always be a Gipsy, travelling light, few possessions. She's working in London at the moment."

"Yes. Your father told me. Patrick's in Canberra with the federal police, and Tess recently married and moved to Perth with her husband."

Beth smiled. "It was a beautiful wedding. Tess looked radiantly happy."

He returned the smile. "Tess was always a delight. So bubbly and game for anything."

"Still is," Beth agreed, comfortable with the conversation about her family. Talking about the familiar took away the edge of facing an intimate stranger.

As she went on eating her meal, enjoying it to the last morsel, memories flooded in and out of her mind. Jamie showing Patrick how best to climb a tree, carrying Kate home when she'd gashed her leg, teaching Tess how to swim. Her brothers and sisters had all looked up to him.

They would look up to him now for the success he had made of his life. Kate would consider him a gorgeous hunk, as well. But what was in the soul of a survivor apart from the scream for all that was unattainable to him? Was she part of that scream? Did he want her to answer it? Or did he want to lay the old part of his life to rest?

When their waiter cleared the table, she sat back and tried to assess the man he had become. He returned her thoughtful gaze, as though assessing her, too. They had shared highly physical intimacies, yet in some strange way, this exchange of words was more deeply intimate, cutting through the years to an understanding that had once needed no words at all.

"All your chicks have flown, Beth," he quietly remarked.

Except Kevin. Who would never fly.

"Is there anything to keep you in Melbourne?"

Danger signals zipped along Beth's nerves. The talk about her family—this was what it had been leading to. Nothing to do with fond memories of the past. He wanted her at the farm with her father. Jim Neilson was a master calculator. Forget Jamie, she harshly berated herself. This was the real world.

He'd been lulling her into a friendly acceptance of him, recalling the old sense of togetherness. The quivery uncertainty seized her again. Was she still chasing a dream with this man, one that had no hope of ever coming true? Was she really prepared to take less in pursuing a need to know?

"I won't be bought," she stated flatly, her eyes flashing a proud warning.

He shook his head. "I wasn't trying to buy you, Beth. Not yesterday or today. I was buying a chance."

"You mean an option, don't you?" She remembered his business. People skilled in trading took out options on things they might want.

"No. An option gives me the choice. It's true I've tried to load the bases my way. But the choice is still yours, Beth."

"Fine. Then I'll choose when I'm ready to." She would not move to his will.

He didn't like it. "What's stopping you?" he asked.

"I don't want you taking anything for granted, Jim Neilson."

He leaned forward, opening his hands in appeal. His eyes blazed with need, with almost chaotic desire, a turbulence of spirit that was infinitely disturbing. Beth tensed and moved away from him, wary of the powerful energy directed at her.

"I'm asking for another chance." Passion swirled from his voice, enveloping her. "Come to the farm with your father. Let me show you another life, Beth. You can always walk away if you don't like it, but let me show you. Will you do that?"

Her mind shrieked caution but her mouth opened and the word came out, drawn from some unguarded place in her soul. "Yes," she heard herself say, and the wild leap of triumph in his eyes, the dazzling smile that erupted caused a weird sense of meltdown inside her, barriers dissolving, heat pumping through her veins, a dizzy feeling of time blurring, showing her a future where what had been impossibilities turned into possibilities.

He'd won, she thought. She'd let him win. But might not she be winning, too?

CHAPTER FOURTEEN

ANOTHER life.

Well, let it begin, Beth decided, and asked him to explain how he ran his business, what hours he worked, what staff he employed, what he actually did, Jim Neilson, this man she was committed to accepting as he was until the feelings they had were resolved.

She had a sketchy idea of his career from the articles she'd read about him. She knew it took nerve and enormous mental strength and agility to balance all the factors in his dealing on the money markets. Now she saw his joy in the game of pitting his judgment against others in the same ballpark, the sparkle in winning, the confidence that winning had given him.

And she saw and felt his pleasure in her interest, the desire to share his world with her, the hopeful reaching out to someone who had cared about him, wanting her to still care despite the mountain of time that had passed. The chance he'd bought. No, the chance he'd made with persistence and passion, refusing to accept defeat.

The chocolate and coffee soufflé came, sheer ambrosia melting in her mouth. For the first time she felt the romance of the restaurant, its appeal to all the senses, the subtle luxury of smoothly attentive but unobtrusive service, the softly inviting intimacy it engendered. *Another life*. The kind of life Jim Neilson could afford to provide. Seductive. But it wouldn't last if the feelings didn't hold true.

She watched his eyes, the windows of his soul. Was Jamie still in there? She willed him to come out. Fiercely. With all the need in her soul.

Jim Neilson stopped talking in mid-sentence. Beth had lost the drift of what he'd been saying, caught up in her private reverie, but she was instantly aware of his sudden silence, of his expression changing.

The eyes that had been dancing stilled, the lights in them swallowed up by a concentrated darkness that was mesmerising in its intensity, as though it led through a tunnel that ended in one of the black holes of the universe. Something stirred in that vast, dark emptiness. It rushed towards her, then was checked, but she sensed its presence, lying in wait, guarded by the will of a man who armoured himself against hurt.

Yes, Beth thought. The scars ran deep. But underneath them, if she could reach beyond them, if he decided to open up to her, there was a chance of getting back at least some of what had been lost. Trust had to work both ways.

"Am I boring you?" he asked.

"Not at all. It's fascinating. I can't help looking for parallels, Jim. I'm sorry if..."

He grinned. "Well, that's an advance."

"Pardon?" He was incredibly handsome with that rakish grin on his face, compellingly attractive.

"Jim is a lot friendlier than the rather pejorative Jim Neilson you've been using."

"Oh!" Heat raced through her veins, blooming into hot patches on her cheeks. "I didn't like you. It felt all wrong," she confessed.

"I know. I hope to improve upon acquaintance," he said dryly.

She laughed, self-consciously pleased he was prepared to dismiss the acrimony she had thrown at him.

He sat back and looked at her with happy eyes. "The Moscow State Circus is coming to Sydney soon. Would you like to go?"

"And see the flying trapeze and high wire acts?" It was what they used to talk about.

He immediately picked up on it. "They can't possibly be as good as we were at swinging on ropes and walking the top palings of the fences, but we could check them out."

"That would be fun," she agreed.

It was so long since she had had any real fun. Frivolous, light-hearted fun. She hoped it was going to be possible, that the tension she felt with him would ease into a more relaxed relationship.

Coffee was served. It was accompanied by a plate of biscotti and a glass of Vin Santo, the waiter explaining this was a very delicate Italian dessert wine into which one dipped the biscuits.

The final exquisite touch to a magnificent dinner, Beth thought appreciatively.

"How long do you think it will be before we can take up residency on the farm?" she asked, remembering why she had agreed to this dinner.

"Do you have a fax machine?"

"Yes." It was handy to have one in the publishing business, allowing for fast correspondence when needed.

"I'll get my solicitor working on the partnership papers tomorrow. All going well, he should be able to push everything through in a week."

She was startled. A week! He wasn't giving her time to have second thoughts, was her first reaction, igniting a spark of resentment. Didn't he trust her to keep to her word?

Then she realised this was characteristic of him, making decisions and acting quickly on them. All the same, she didn't have to move at his pace. She thought of how she worked, her mind in a dream, often forgetting mealtimes and other household chores, like leaving the laundered clothes in the washing machine for hours instead of remembering to transfer them to the dryer. Would he understand the weird ways of the creative process and make allowances for them?

"I thought properties usually took six weeks or so for the paperwork to get done," she said, starting to consider the thousand and one things that would have to be done in closing up their lives in Melbourne.

"My solicitor is paid to be very efficient."

Beth received the strong impression Jim Neilson didn't tolerate inefficiency. Probably in his world he couldn't afford to. He would want instant service, instant information, instant responses, and he would make sure he got what he paid for. She wondered how demanding he would be in his private life, what expectations he would have of her.

"Is a week too soon for you to move, Beth?" he asked. Then as though realising he might be pressuring her, quickly added. "Take whatever time you need."

It was a daunting operation, saying goodbye to one life to start another. What would she be leaving behind? Her mother's and Kevin's graves were here. But their spirits were somewhere else. Some better place, she told herself. The rest of her family had gone. It was time to move on, anyway. Hadn't she decided that, even before Jim Neilson had entered her life?

A line from Shakespeare's *Macbeth* came back to her—"If it were done when 'tis done, then 'twere well it were done quickly."

"Dad will be eager to go," she said out loud. Then decisively, "We'll come as soon as everything's organised."

He looked pleased. "I'll have a caravan on the property by next weekend. Or would you prefer to choose one yourself?"

She shook her head. "The caravan is only a temporary measure. It won't be long before the house is habitable. Having it properly rewired is the first priority. Phone, fax, computer... I need them working."

"I'll line that up for you."

And would be completely dependable about making such arrangements, Beth thought. If Jim Neilson said he was going to do something, it would get done. Jamie had been like that, too. No excuses. That was one of the reasons she had found it so difficult to accept his failure to keep his word about coming to her in Melbourne.

Sadness swept through her, all the years of unnecessary separation dragging at her heart. She hadn't even known about that turning point in her life, hadn't been given the chance to change Jamie's mind about it. This was another turning point. To another life. If it didn't work out as she hoped it would... Well, at least she would have tried.

"Something wrong, Beth?" Jim asked.

She heaved a sigh to relieve the constriction in her chest. "Just thinking how strange things are. I meant to say goodbye to you tonight."

"I know."

"And now I'm going back to the valley of our childhood. And you'll be there, too, when you can be." She eyed him consideringly. "Will it be a hardship for you, returning to those memories?"

"I have good memories, too. Of you, Beth," he said softly.

"We're not the same people," she reminded him.

"No. But I see a chance that we'll find what we were."

Was that hope talking? She searched his eyes intently as she said, "They say one should never go back."

"Maybe it's necessary."

He was determined on it, no matter what the outcome. She gave him a wry smile. "I guess we can only try."

He nodded. "Otherwise we'll never know."

She felt his inner turmoil, too, the yearning, the questioning, the uncertainty, the need. Could they cross the barrier of time and link hands again in trust and confidence and love?

"When are you flying back to Sydney?" she asked.

"First flight in the morning."

"You're staying overnight somewhere."

He nodded. "The Hotel Como in South Yarra."

She checked her watch. It was almost eleven-thirty. There was no more to settle between them. The die was cast. "We should get moving. You won't get much sleep."

He didn't argue. He settled the bill with a credit card, undoubtedly adding lavish tips. The maître d' asked if he wanted a taxi called. The decision was to see her to her car first.

It was something of a shock walking out of the warm magic of the restaurant to the bleak, impersonal coldness of Lonsdale Street. It was more of a shock when her hand was caught and held, strong, warm fingers lacing through hers in a grip that had no intention of losing possession. She didn't try to pull away. It would have been a ridiculous rejection, given the far more intimate connections they had shared. Yet somehow this link was more meaningful, reforging the most childish physical link there was, holding hands. Beth was acutely conscious of it.

He paced his footsteps to match hers, walking beside her in a silence that seemed to hum with old memories of friendship and togetherness. The beat of their shoes on the pavement had an eerie echo of timelessness. Were they walking a new path or simply a different dimension of a path forged long ago?

They reached her car. His grip tightened slightly before letting go so she could extract her keys from her handbag. She was extremely conscious of him waiting beside her. A man, not a boy. A man whose strong sexuality had moved her into a deeper knowledge of her own. Those wild journeys with him raced through her mind as she unlocked the car and opened the driver's door.

"I'm glad you came to see me, Beth."

His voice was low, intense, furred with feelings she instantly recognised as physical as well as emotional. It drew her gaze to his, and their eyes locked in a steamy stream of unspoken desire.

"I'm glad, too," she said. It was true. Honesty was important now. For trust there had to be honesty between them. And the truth was she didn't want to leave him here in the street. She wanted... "It's not far out of my way to your hotel. Would you like a lift?"

"Yes. Thank you."

Am I mad? she wondered as he settled on the seat beside her. In the closeness of the car she could smell his cologne. All her senses were heightened. One glance at his legs and she didn't see the black fabric of his trousers. She saw the powerfully muscled thighs underneath it. Her heart was thundering in her ears.

Drive, her mind commanded. Her hands obeyed, switching on the ignition. Her feet worked the pedals automatically. She tried to think with some modicum of common sense. Wouldn't it be better to hold back, be more circumspect in pursuing this relationship with Jim Neilson? She already knew they were sexually compatible. It was their compatibility in other areas of their lives that had to be determined. But all her furious thinking did nothing to ease the fine tension of anticipation zinging through her body.

They travelled in silence. She didn't even notice he made no attempt at conversation until they were driving down Chapel Street, almost at the hotel. Suddenly she realised he had to be thinking along the same lines she was. What conclusion had he come to? Would he effect a polite farewell or push for something more? If the latter, how should she respond?

She slowed the car to take the turn into the driveway that led to the entrance door of the hotel. Still no word from him. Through the glass frontage she saw the concierge paying attention to their arrival. She brought the car to a halt under the portico, leaving the engine idling. A lift was a lift. She hadn't suggested anything more than that, yet her nerves were screaming for more.

He made no move to alight. His stillness goaded her to look at him. She constructed a smile. Her mind dictated the words *good night*. She turned her head and was totally swamped by the blaze of raw wanting in his eyes.

"Will you come up to my room with me, Beth?" he asked quietly, the control in his voice assuring her he would respect her reply, whichever way it went.

An invitation.

The choice was hers.

Would it be the same as before . . . or different?

The temptation to know was overwhelming.

"Yes," she said huskily, and switched off the engine.

CHAPTER FIFTEEN

WHERE did it begin, the soaring sense of true togetherness?

With the first kiss?

The restraint of it?

He cupped her face, a faint quiver in the long, warm fingers stroking the soft skin of her cheeks, his eyes dark whirlpools drawing her down the years to long ago, needing to reach back for the feeling that had once been theirs. He kissed her as though she was infinitely precious, with slow, exquisite tenderness, almost fearful that something fragile might be dislodged or bruised or tarnished if he didn't take the greatest care, the first kiss of another life, knowing what had been lost. Lost—not devalued or wilfully tossed away or forgotten.

The grieving for it was in their mouths, the yearning for it, the hope for it, the tentative seeking for it. A boy and girl who'd created their own world, a mixture of reality and dreams of tomorrow that had always carried the certainty of sharing it, inconceivable for them not to, somehow, some way... Beth and Jamie.

Was tomorrow here at last for them? Could it be?

They hugged as they had once hugged in promising themselves to each other, her arms tightly around his waist, not wanting to let go, afraid of the unknown without him, her head on his shoulder, fighting the tears in her eyes because she had to be brave, his cheek rubbing against her hair, comforting, loving, and the memory of the words he'd spoken whispering through her mind.

"I'll come to you, Beth. As soon as I can I'll come to you. And one day there'll be nothing to part us. Ever again."

One day...

He was with her now, remembering, though this time he moved his mouth over her hair, trailing warm kisses, and his body was that of a man, fully grown and aroused with wanting the woman she had become, wanting the intimacy adults knew, the physical bonding that took them beyond the innocence of childhood and into the reality of meeting each other on this first night of their future.

So strange, the sense of a journey of discovery as they shed their clothes, like a slow peeling away of layers of protection, letting go the armour in more than a physical sense, keenly conscious of who they were to each other now and laying themselves bare to the vision of something more than either of them.

Immaterial that they had been naked together only two nights ago. This was a different experience. The revelation that there had been no betrayal from either of them injected a feeling of awe, of wonderment, a joy so deep it couldn't be voiced lest it be somehow fractured. The feeling of vulnerability was strong, yet thrilling, too, because they were both risking all they were for what might be.

Such exquisite tension in the touching, gentle caresses heightening sensitivity, cherishing, loving, revelling in the flesh-and-blood warmth of a dream that hadn't died, that could be resurrected if they cared enough, believed enough, wanted enough. The barrier of time was meaningless in this hour of knowing each other again.

A more needful kiss, simmering with barely leashed passion for the ultimate joining, their bodies straining to give and take, intensely aware there was something to be proved, the desire for it coursing through them, demanding fulfilment of the promise yet quivering on the edge of it, knowing the final plunge would mean so much— perhaps too much.

But it had to come.

Determination was in the hard, manly strength of the arms that lifted her and cradled her against the heaving muscles of his broad chest. A blaze of possession was in his eyes, the fierce intention to make her his woman. And she curled her arms around his neck, exulting in his resolution, wanting this man to be her man, the only one ever.

A soft Doona under her back, soft pillows under her head, her legs openly inviting him, her hands still linked behind his neck, their eyes locked, swimming in a tumultuous sea of feeling as he poised himself above her, and he whispered her name, like a soft call from his soul, a beat of his heart, a brand on his body.

Then it came, the full shaft of his manhood sliding inside her, slowly easing forward, feeling the throb of her welcome, her need of him, the sweet inner path of a woman who wanted all he could give, savouring the sensation of him moving deeper, deeper, filling the empty place that had been waiting, waiting it seemed for eternity, waiting for him to complete what had never been completed.

For a moment her heart suspended its beat, her body hung on a pinnacle of anticipation, her soul quivered with excitement, her eyes clung to his as her mind cried, *Let it be, let it be* ... And she heard, sensed, felt the silent scream from him, *Yes*, and there he was. Yes...the need in his mind meshing with hers, tunneling down, down, bursting into her soul as he touched her womb, the deep, magical touch of mating, the physical recognition of their lives melding in a union that was uniquely theirs, and a sigh of blissful contentment rippled through her at the rightness of it ... yes.

Was it then the soaring began? The celebration of that ecstatic moment repeated and repeated in the rhythm of togetherness?

It was so beautiful, like a cup being filled and filled with the best this life had to offer, until it overflowed in an exquisite explosion of sensation that lifted them beyond physical things, into a stream of communion that obliterated every level of separation, and they were one in spirit again.

Or so it felt.

The huge emotional swell could not be contained. Tears gushed into Beth's eyes. She was gently wrapped in his arms, carried with him to lie with her head over the soothing drum of his heart, and he held her tightly to him, stroking her hair as she sobbed out the relief of this coming together and the grief of having been parted for so long.

Eventually she quietened, the strong assurance of his possessive embrace and the tender caring in his continual caressing seeping through her, promising it wasn't over and it wasn't a dream. It was real and true and it wasn't going to stop here.

The tears had washed away the pain of the past.

This was a new beginning.

The future was theirs to make of it what they would.

And she wanted it to go on like this . . . forever.

Let it be, she silently prayed.

Let it be.

CHAPTER SIXTEEN

SAM'S excited barking and prancing were the first signals. Beth smiled, her heart lifting with happiness as she pressed the save button on the keyboard and rose from the chair in front of her computer. No sooner had she opened the door onto the veranda than the labrador pup shot out to perform his eager welcome routine. She could hear it now, too, the distinctive sound of the Porsche burning up the valley road to the farm.

"Jim's here, Aunty Em," she called into the house.

"I'm just icing the cake. Tell him it's his favourite, chocolate sponge made with eggwhites."

Beth grinned. Jim was always a good excuse to produce a masterpiece. Aunty Em had strongly advised against replacing the old Aga cooker in the kitchen for something more modern. For cake-making, nothing could beat it, and since she was spending more time at the farm with her brother than at her granny flat in Ryde, nobody was about to argue over what she wanted in the kitchen. Aunty Em was definitely in her element with good, old-fashioned equipment.

The Porsche dropped its revs to turn into the property. Sam was tearing towards the gateway.

He was supposedly Beth's dog, Jim having presented him to her the first week after she and her father had arrived here, but the eight-week-old puppy had already decided that the man who'd bought him was his real master. Or, as Aunty Em said, Jim and dogs had a natural affinity.

Beth started down the front steps, thinking how much had been achieved over the past two and a half months. Even the garden was in technicolour bloom for Christmas, only ten days away. She glanced at the pile of timber waiting for Jim's arrival. He was going to help her father put up the picket fence this weekend. Once that was done and painted, the place would really look like home again.

Her father was anxious to have everything right for Christmas. Chris and Patrick were coming. And last night, a phone call from Kate to say she was flying home, too. Tess couldn't be here. She would be with her husband's family in Perth. But for the most part, it would be like old times again. With her father very much his former self, and Jim sharing it with them, the happy memories would flow.

Dog and car made a race of it to the house. Jim alighted, laughing as Sam leapt on him, ready to lick every available part of the man he loved. Beth's love for him welled up as she watched them together, pleasure written so openly on Jim's face. He didn't mind coming here at all. He enjoyed discussing plans with her father, acting on them. And in his eyes, whenever he looked at her, no holding back the wanting for everything to be right between them.

It was there now as he watched her coming to greet him, such a warm blaze of feeling enveloping her, tugging her to him. He didn't move to meet her. She felt him drinking in the sight of her. Then she was in his arms, and he was drinking in the taste of her, the feel of her. And the magic of being together flowed again.

"I brought something back to you," he said, releasing her to duck into the car and pick up a book from the passenger seat. "I thought you'd like to have it again now."

Her heart turned over as he passed it to her, the book she'd given him fifteen years ago, with her address in Melbourne written on the flyleaf.

"I know it was your favourite," he added softly.

Black Beauty. A gift from her mother on her tenth birthday. She had loved the story, treasured the book, lent it to Jamie so he could read it and share her pleasure in it. When they had to part, there had been nothing more precious to give him as a keepsake.

Her eyes blurred with tears as she stared at this link with the past, to the time before Jim had lost faith in her feeling for him. The cover was slightly tattered and spotted, the marks of having travelled far and been in many places, taken with him wherever he went. She swallowed hard to ease the lump in her throat and raised her eyes to his.

"Why did you hold onto it?"

He lifted his hand to her cheek, gently brushing the trickle of moisture at the corner of her eye. "I couldn't let go of the memory. The dream was shattered, Beth, but not the memory of you as you were to me then. That was always precious."

"Yes. Always precious," she echoed huskily. "Thank you for giving it back to me."

He smiled. "I have no need of it any more."

His eyes said she was all he needed now.

Beth hugged that thought all day.

The weather was mild, sunny without being too hot for working. Jim and her father had all the fence posts in by lunchtime. Aunty Em served a hearty meal of roast beef. Putting the railings up took most of the afternoon. Her father then declared they'd done enough, and tomorrow was soon enough to start on the picket palings. They retired to sit on the veranda and relax over a few beers before cleaning up for dinner.

It said a lot for Jim's sensitivity that he was prepared to work alongside her father rather than calling in a team of fencing contractors to do the labouring for him. That wouldn't have sat well with Tom Delaney. This way the partnership felt right to him. They were building something together.

They shared an easygoing rapport with respect on both sides, mutually satisfying in lots of ways. Jim had never had a father, and his relationship with Beth made him almost like a son to her dad. It wasn't likely her brothers would return to the land, not in any lifestyle sense. Jim provided a sense of continuity.

Filling needs.

Was that what love was all about?

She had worried about meeting Jim's expectations, but he didn't seem to have any of her. He seemed perfectly content to simply have her with him. Twice she'd spent a week in Sydney, staying in his penthouse. He'd taken her to the Moscow Circus and to the theatre to see musicals and plays—whatever took her fancy. Wonderful nights together, sharing pleasure.

During the days she could use his personal computer in his study to work as she pleased while he attended to his business. There was no friction between them about anything. He enjoyed listening to her talk about what she was writing. He said it was a great escape from his high-pressure world.

Perhaps the farm was, too. For a man who'd lived a very solitary life, the family atmosphere had to be attractive. And Aunty's Em's home cooking was always a treat. She produced a wonderful steak and kidney pie for dinner, and Jim polished off his helping with much vocal appreciation. Her aunt beamed with pleasure. She was only too happy to usher him and Beth out for an evening walk, insisting she and Tom would do the dishes.

Sam accompanied them, eager for adventure. They followed the creek until they came to the track that cut through the back of the valley to old Jorgen's farm. Jim steered her onto it, holding her hand firmly in his. Beth glanced apprehensively at him, concerned about the memories such a walk would stir.

"Are you sure you want to go this way, Jim?"

He gave her a reassuring smile. "Time to lay ghosts to rest, Beth."

"If you say so," she murmured uncertainly. She knew Jorgen had died many years ago. The farmhouse had burnt down, and he'd burnt with it. A fitting end, she'd thought, for a man who'd dished out hell to Jamie. But that still didn't make it a good place to visit.

"He didn't make a will," Jim said dryly. "Some time after his death, I was notified that I was the only living heir. Apparently my mother had died of a drug overdose, so the property came to me. Ironic, isn't it?"

Sad, she thought. "Did you ever try to find your mother?"

"No. She knew what she was leaving me to. It was what she'd run away from."

Beth shook her head. "I don't know how she could have done it."

"Out of spite. She'd lived with Jorgen saying she should have been a son. So she gave him one." He shrugged. "If she was taking drugs she probably wasn't in her right mind."

"I guess not." All the same, abandoning her child to a bitter old tyrant was unforgivable to Beth. Though if it hadn't been done, she and

Jamie might never have met. She heaved a rueful sigh and asked, "Have you sold the property?"

"No. I didn't want to touch it. I wanted it to rot into nothing."

Dust to dust, she thought.

"I finally realised this week I was still hanging onto it instead of letting it go. So I gave it away."

That startled her. "To whom?"

His grin flashed with intense satisfaction. "An organisation that helps kids who've been kicked in the guts by life. It gets them on their feet again."

"What a great idea!" She warmly approved.

It was not only letting the bad memories go, but completely turning around what the place had meant to him.

"I got rid of the Brett Whitely painting, too. Gave it to Claud to sell for me."

"Why?" She was utterly astonished, but glad. It was not a painting she would ever have chosen to live with.

"You didn't like it."

"It pulsed with pain," she said quietly, unable to deny her dislike.

"It used to suit my more savage moods." He grinned at her. "Having you soothes the beast in me."

She laughed, her eyes twinkling teasingly. "I don't mind a bit of savage sometimes."

Desire instantly kindled. "If Sam wasn't with us, I'd be severely tempted to take you up on that."

Hearing his name, the dog frolicked around them, barking for attention. Sam would definitely try to get in on the act of lovemaking, trying to nudge between them and lick their faces. Much better to wait until they were alone and could concentrate completely on each other. Tonight was soon enough.

This walk was good, Beth decided, shedding the baggage of the past. Nevertheless, she was conscious of a growing tension in Jim as they approached the boundary fence of what had been the prison of his childhood and adolescence. Resolutions were great in principle. Facing painful memories was not so easy.

They reached the sliprails where they used to say goodbye to each other. Beth had not been welcome on Jorgen's farm. No one was. Jim released her hand. She hesitated, not knowing if he wanted her to go on with him.

But he didn't climb through the fence. He leaned his arms on the top railing and slowly surveyed the scene of his former misery. Beth stepped beside him, keeping a silent vigil as he looked his fill.

In the gathering twilight, the property had an abandoned, decaying air. The remnants of a blackened brick chimney stood where the house had been. The dairy and barn were only fit for demolition, their roofs half gone, their walls with large sections either rotted away or fallen askew. The fields were full of thistles, occasionally broken by piles of rocks Jim had humped out of the way so the ground could be ploughed. Old machinery had been left to rust, half-buried in weeds.

"After you'd gone to Melbourne, I used to come and stand here at night, when Jorgen had gone to bed," he said quietly. "It made me feel close to you."

So lonely, bereft of any love. She moved to stand behind him, sliding her arms around his waist, hugging him, laying her head on his shoulder. "I'm sorry you didn't get my letters," she murmured.

"In a way, it was better not getting them, Beth. I didn't want to know about your life away from me. I used to stand here and relive what we'd shared, dream about a future when we'd be together again. That way you were still mine. You didn't belong anywhere else."

Still mine. Until he'd seen her with Kevin. "When you left here, did you think of writing to me?" she asked softly, wanting to know more of those years that were dark to her.

"No. I had nothing good to tell you. Nothing I could even promise you with any real confidence."

Pride. The need for a sense of self-worth before reaching out for her.

"I stuck it out here until I had my school certificate. It gave me something to start with. To build on. I took whatever jobs I could get in Sydney and enrolled at college part time. It was all work, lectures, study, living as cheaply as possible.''

He turned to face her, leaning against the fence, drawing her between his legs to hold her close. His eyes sought her understanding. ''You know what that course is like, Beth. You did it, too, in between looking after your family.''

''No time for play,'' she said, sympathetically aware of the struggle to make it through.

''I aimed for a scholarship at the business college. I knew that would lead me into the financial world with the proper qualifications.'' His eyes flashed an appeal. ''When you've had nothing, the idea of making a lot of money is...quite compelling.''

She knew what the lack of money was like. Her father had lost the farm because of it, and they'd lived hand to mouth during those early years in Melbourne, barely making do.

''I worked all hours and saved all I could in case I didn't get the scholarship,'' he went on, intensity creeping into his voice. ''I had to get those qualifications one way or another. But the scholarship came through a week before the first term was to start.''

''That must have been a marvellous moment,'' she said, smiling with pride in him.

He didn't smile back. His eyes were full of pain as he said, ''That's when I came to you, Beth. I felt I finally had a grasp on a future. I threw in my jobs and came down to Melbourne to tell you.''

Her smile died. She could imagine his jubilance, the exhilarating anticipation of sharing his achievement with her. To have all those wonderful, positive feelings dashed...

"It was the first week in February," he went on. "By the time I got to the address you'd given me, it was too late to catch you before you went to school. Though it didn't really matter. I was happy to wander around the area where you lived, imagining how it was for you."

"Why didn't you knock on our door?"

"I wanted to see you first. I liked your family, but you—you were all-important to me. I imagined it so many ways, how your eyes would light up and you'd run to me, dropping everything so we could hug. And I'd twirl you around and we'd laugh and be deliriously happy. And you'd be so much more grown up at sixteen. We could plan our future together."

Young romantic dreams. Her heart wept for them. For her own, too, dying their long, slow death.

He sighed, and there was darkly remembered torment in his eyes as he said, "When I saw you with Kevin—at first, I couldn't believe it. You weren't at school. You had a baby."

The bottom dropping out of his world, making chaos of it. Beth could see—feel—how devastating that moment had been to him.

"I'd never even looked at another girl, Beth," he pleaded softly. "There was only you."

"It's all right," she soothed, no forgiveness necessary. "I understand how it was for you. If I'd seen you even hugging some other girl, I would have felt the same."

He sadly shook his head. "All I could think of was...it wasn't my baby. You'd had a child with someone else."

The ultimate betrayal.

The three years apart had created a gap for damage to be done. If there'd been communication between them, letters...

"Knowing what I do now," he went on regretfully, "I should have confronted the situation, spoken to you, instead of walking away. All I can say is, something inside me broke that day. I couldn't face it, Beth."

Something inside me broke.

It was Jamie, her Jamie who had broken.

And Jim Neilson had emerged from the wreckage.

She reached up and stroked the cheek of the man who was now both Jamie and Jim, her eyes assuring him there was no diminishment in her love for him. "It's behind us. It happened. It's gone. We found each other again. That's a miracle, isn't it?"

He looked relieved at her simple acceptance of the present. His face relaxed. His eyes glowed with love for her. "Will you marry me, Beth? Share the future with me?" he asked softly.

"You know I will," she answered, her heart almost bursting with happiness.

"Always and forever?" he asked, echoing words said long ago, two children forging an eternal bond that neither would ever let go.

"Always and forever," she repeated huskily.

Beth and Jamie, Jamie and Beth.

They kissed.

And the bond was complete.

Above them, in a sky filling with stars, a full moon was rising.

CHAPTER SEVENTEEN

SHE wore yellow.

A garland of daisies in her golden hair, a posy of daisies in her hand.

She was sunshine and summer and all the warm things of life.

Her father walked her towards him. Her brother Chris stood at his side.

The words of a poem came to him, one recited and learnt long ago in the valley schoolroom.

This be the verse you engrave for me:
Here he lies where he longed to be;
Home is the sailor, home from the sea,
And the hunter home from the hill.

She stepped beside him and gave him her hand. In just a few minutes they would exchange golden rings, tokens of the formal bond they were about to declare. But her hand was enough.

He had come home.

On the plus side, you've raised a
wonderful, strong-willed daughter.
On the minus side, she's using that
determination to find

A Match For
MOM

Three very different stories of mothers,
daughters and heroes...from three of your
all-time favorite authors:

GUILTY
by Anne Mather

A MAN FOR MOM
by Linda Randall Wisdom

THE FIX-IT MAN
by Vicki Lewis Thompson

Available this May wherever
Harlequin and Silhouette books are sold.

 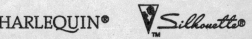

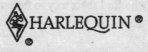